One Night in Paris

ELLIS ROSE

Second Edition Published in 2016
by iponymous publishing Limited
iponymous Swansea United Kingdom SA6 6BP

A CIP record for this book
Is available from the British Library

(Physical Book) ISBN 978-1-908773-07-4
(EBook) ISBN 978-1-908773-27-2

www.iponymous.com

ALSO BY ELLIS ROSE

One Night in Paris

Another Night in Paris

Last Night in Paris

CONTENTS

ELLIS ROSE

Originally from Swansea in South Wales, Ellis Rose, studied modern languages at Cardiff University before moving to Paris to follow a career in Public Relations. After 30 years of working in a variety of marketing and PR related roles in Europe and the UK, in 2009 she moved back to her home town where she set up her own independent marketing consultancy, to allow herself time to write her first novel. Ellis now lives with her partner and two daughters on the beautiful Gower Coast.

CHAPTER 1

Three in a bed! This was not Josie's idea of a good start to the New Year. She knew where she was, whose bed she was in and who was in it with her. Knowing this didn't make her feel any better.

Forcing her mind through a major hangover haze, she tried to piece together the events of the night before – New Year's Eve.

Her friend Angie had come to visit her in Paris for the New Year where Josie had lived and worked for the past 6 months. Her flatmate, Chrissie, had gone home for Christmas and New Year, so it had seemed like a good idea to have Angie to stay. Josie didn't really like staying in the flat on her own and when Angie asked what her plans were for New Year it seemed like a good idea to invite her to Paris for a few days. She had spent a relatively quiet week with her family at home in Bristol, recovering from the hectic and excessive build up to Christmas that the girls had enjoyed.

In addition to their respective office parties, Josie and Chrissie had been invited to far too many other do's and by the time they headed for Charles de Gaulle airport on their way back to the UK, both girls felt the need for a rest from their heady Parisian lifestyle.

"Our party was the best though," Chrissie said to Josie as they jostled their way down the overcrowded carriages of the Métro with their suitcases.

They had invited all of their office colleagues as well as mutual friends though word must have spread as total strangers turned up too. The party extended out onto the corridor of their flat and then down onto the street, much to their neighbours' annoyance. The revelling came to an end with the timely arrival of the gendarmes but even a week after the event, both girls' friends didn't stop talking about it.

"I agree," replied Josie, "it must be a British thing because most of the other parties were a bit one-sided when it came to the men enjoying themselves and the women looking on from the sidelines. I must say French women can be particularly boring. They hardly drink and most of them look pretty sour faced when their men are having a good time.... it must be a cultural thing?"

Chrissie laughed, "It's no wonder we're so popular at parties. At least we know how to have a good time."

They parted company at the airport as Josie's flight was earlier than Chrissie's who's family lived in London. "I'm going to take it easy at home," Josie told her friend as they kissed goodbye.

"Me too," replied Chrissie. "My liver needs a rest. Merry Christmas Josie and see you next year!"

After a week with her family and her mum in particular fussing over her, Josie was ready to come back to Paris. She arranged to meet Angie at Charles de Gaulle airport on the day before New Year's Eve so that they could travel back to the flat together.

They'd only been back for a day before Angie had began to get on Josie's nerves. "I'd forgotten how sex crazed she was," she thought when for what seemed like the twentieth time Angie asked how she looked, who would be at the club for the party, who was available, would they fancy her and would it be OK to bring someone home.

They had met two years ago in Switzerland. Both girls were language students working in the popular Swiss ski resort of Crans Montana during their placement year abroad. They had kept in touch and the following year Angie had come to stay for another New Year with Josie's family in the UK.

They had gone out to Café Valance, a local restaurant where lots of her friends hung out and which was renowned for a good New Year's bash. Josie lived on the outskirts of Bristol in an area called Chipping Sodbury. Most of her school friends, like her, were away at college at the time but they had all agreed to meet again at their favourite teenage party venue in the quirky village of Clifton.

Her father dropped the girls off at the restaurant and slipped Josie £20 for a taxi home.

"Have a good time girls," he said as they climbed out of the car, smoothing down their hair and clothes as a sudden gust of wind blew up around them, playing havoc with all the hours of pampering and preparation.

Josie was greeted by her female and male friends who were already at the party and she introduced Angie to them all, explaining how they met during their year abroad from college.

Angie asked Josie lots of questions about all the different males who were there and within half an hour, she had disappeared into the loo with Edmund, the younger brother of Josie's school friend Marcus. Emerging a while later, Angie proudly announced that she was off with 'young' Ed and would be back before midnight.

"You'd better be," said Josie. "My mum will go mental if I go home without you."

Angie did make it back by midnight and then spent the rest of the evening and the next day going into graphic details of her romp with 'young' Ed.

So it seemed like the evening ahead might very well follow a similar pattern. "Never again," said Josie under her breath as Angie launched into another tirade of questions about Daniel, their 'escort' for the evening.

"Is he hot?" she asked. "You've told me he's rich and his house sounds wonderful but is he hot?"

Now 'hot' is not a word Josie necessarily associated with Daniel.

"Desperate more like," she replied enjoying the look of disappointment on Angie's face. "He's been trying to get into Chrissie's pants for months with no luck. She knows how to play him though. He'll do anything she asks in the hope that one day she'll give in. Poor Daniel, he's got no chance."

Josie in fact thought Daniel was a nice man. He was kind and considerate but besotted by her flat mate Chrissie and just couldn't see that she was leading him on. A few years before he had endured a particularly nasty divorce and since then it seemed he hadn't had much luck with new relationships. So he did come over as a bit desperate as far as women were concerned. He was always recommending trips and treats to Chrissie who more often than not agreed, provided Josie and their friend Libby came along too.

He was an accountant in the European office of an

international bank and was quite well off. Unfortunately he wasn't very good looking. He was a bit overweight, with pale skin, sandyish hair and a sort of two tone moustache which didn't sit quite right on his face.

"You'll see for yourself in a minute anyway,' said Josie. "I expect that's him now."

Josie pressed the intercom to the flat to let Daniel in. His fashion sense wasn't up to much either; he was wearing baggy beige cords, brown brogues and a brown and green checked shirt. Not standard New Year's Eve party attire in either girl's eyes.

"Angie Daniel, Daniel Angie," said Josie noticing the disappointment on Angie's face and the pleasure on Daniel's. In fact he was practically drooling as he admired Angie's appearance. She was a good looking girl, if not a bit too polished. Glossy dark hair cut into a sleek bob with bright blue eyes, a soft, round face, full red mouth, slender neck leading to over exposed pert breasts, small waist and long, slim legs. She was wearing a short tight mini skirt and glossy tights that showed off her slim legs and pert bottom.

Introductions over, Josie poured them all a glass of Kir Royale and toasted the evening ahead. The plans were to go for a meal in their favourite haunt, a small restaurant at Palais Royal called the Le Vieil Ecu and then onto the British Tennis and Cricket Club at Meudon, just outside Paris, to see the New Year in.

Le Vieil Ecu was a bijoux of a restaurant offering a reasonably priced set menu as well as à la carte. Josie usually opted for their signature dish of snails in a strong garlic sauce, mopped up with a basket-full of baguette. But as it was New Year's Eve she had already decided against this option as she didn't want to reek of garlic at the party.

Daniel had volunteered to drive so once they'd a polished off a few Kir Royales, they set off in his car to the restaurant. Not short of money, he drove a BMW soft top convertible which obviously impressed the hell out of Angie.

"Nice car," Angie said as Josie stood back to let her friend get into the back.

"Charming," thought Josie, "Daniel's my friend and yet she's automatically assumed she's sitting in the front."

Josie knew this was childish but couldn't help but feel peeved at Angie's assumption.

The drive to Palais Royal took only a few minutes as the traffic was light and Daniel managed to find a parking space practically outside the restaurant.

"Expecting a good turn-out at the club tonight?" asked Josie once they were seated at their table.

"Oh the usual crowd," replied Daniel, taking in the sight of Angie swaying across the restaurant on her way to the loo.

"She's something else isn't she Josie, does she have a man in her life?"

"Several, I should imagine," replied Josie sharply. "Look Dan, she's only here for a couple of days and, I know she's a friend and all that, but she is a bit of a man eater. I'm just warning you that's all – as a mate!"

But Daniel paid no attention.

"So who from the usual crowd then?" persisted Josie. She was desperate to know if Max was going to be there and, more importantly, if his girlfriend Anna was going to be there too.

"Oh you know. Paul, Jane, Max. All that crowd," he replied.

A wave of relief washed over her. At least Max would be there and even if his girlfriend was there too, they still might manage a snatched moment.

Josie knew she was behaving foolishly when it came to Max. But he was everything she'd ever wanted in a man. He wasn't too tall or too stocky, just a perfect build with dark curly hair and deep blue eyes. He had a good job, his own flat and the sex was out of this world.

Josie had met Max a few months before when she and Chrissie had gone with Daniel to the Tour de L'Arc de Triomphe at the Longchamps racecourse. Daniel had taken along a superb picnic with all the 'French niceties' he knew the girls would enjoy including a crate of champagne. Like many of the other race goers on that day, they had set up the picnic at the back of the car adjacent to the race course so they could see the races easily. They'd all had a few gentle flutters and were getting quite merry.

During the afternoon, Daniel introduced the girls to a group of his British friends who, like him, were members of the tennis and cricket club at Meudon – and one of them was Max. They joined them for more champagne and Josie found herself sitting next to him. It had been lust at first sight. He seemed pretty taken himself and she was glad she'd made the effort with her appearance that morning.

As the day progressed, Max flirted outrageously with Josie who flirted outrageously right back. As the races came to an end and everyone started packing up, Josie invited their new friends back to the girls' flat. Her ulterior motive was to spend more time with Max.

"You can come with me in my car to show me the way, if you like," Max said to Josie as they were packing up Daniel's picnic and chairs.

"OK that's fine, I'll just tell the others," she replied.

In the car Max turned to Josie, "Would you mind stopping off at my place on the way, it's not too far from yours and I can pick up some wine and beer."

"Fine," said Josie, relishing the thought of spending as much time as possible alone with this gorgeous man. They chatted easily and the journey passed quickly despite the queues of traffic leaving the racecourse.

Max lived in a modern block of flats in Belleville, just a few Métro stops away from Josie's own flat behind the Gare St Lazare. He parked outside and asked Josie if she wanted to come up. "Try and stop me," she thought.

In the flat, Max closed the door and instantly put his arms around Josie. "I've been desperate to do this all day," he said and kissed her so passionately that she felt her knees begin to buckle.

Josie was keen on kissing. She hated men who instantly stuck their tongues in your mouth as though they were trying to play a tune on your tonsils. She loved the feel of mouth against mouth, soft at first and then more demanding, until it was OK to start exploring with tongues, gently of course. As far as she was concerned, Max could have written the manual on kissing.

After what seemed like hours, he eventually stopped and stepped back from Josie, keeping his hands lightly on her waist.

"You really are incredibly sexy," he said, drinking in her appearance from top to toe.

"So are you," she replied, and cursed herself for sounding so twee.

He took her hand and led her into the sitting room and pulled her down next to him on a soft, leather sofa. This was the first time Josie had time to look at the apartment properly. The décor was very male and minimalist, mainly white with a smattering of black and grey with very modern furniture. The huge sitting room led onto a kitchen and there was a stunning balcony overlooking Paris which ran the entire length of the room.

Turning her gaze back to Max, she could see instantly what he had in mind and knew she wouldn't be able to resist even if she wanted to.

He began kissing her again and this time explored her neck, her ears, even the corners of her mouth. "I really want to make love to you," he said. Josie couldn't bring herself to reply, so just kissed him back with a passion equal to his own.

She couldn't believe the sensations running through her. It felt as though her body was completely detached from her mind, with a will of its own. Josie knew it was too soon. They'd only met a few hours ago. But it seemed so right, so perfect and she wanted him as much as he wanted her. "It's only sex," she said to herself as Max began to undo her shirt and bra, kissing her breasts as if they were some treasured possession.

Josie allowed herself to flow with the pleasures and sensations Max was creating. Her legs felt shaky and she could practically feel her clitoris hitting the soft lace of her knickers.

"I am going to come as soon as he touches me there," she though as Max began to remove her boots and trousers.

Leaving on her skimpy, lacy underwear, Max started to undo his trouser belt. Josie stopped him and pulled him to his feet.

"Allow me," she said and began slowly unbuttoning his shirt. She slipped this off his shoulders and then began kissing his neck, his shoulders and his nipples. His groans of pleasure told her all she needed to know. She expertly undid his trousers and slipped her hand down inside his boxers.

Feeling the tip of his hard, erect penis against the palm of her hand, Josie wasn't disappointed.

"Thanks goodness for that," she thought to herself, "I would have died if he'd have turned out to have a wee little willy."

There is often a difficult embarrassing moment when a man and woman undress each other – which usually results in him standing there with his trousers and pants around his ankles and his socks still on. Not the case with Max. He somehow managed to lose all his clothes in one fell swoop and stood in front of Josie, strong and proud and very, very erect.

Josie sunk to her knees, holding Max's swollen penis in her

hand. She began to gently lick the tip, running her tongue around the head and then the length of his shaft. For the second time in a few minutes, Max groaned. Josie took as much of him in her mouth as she could, alternating between sucking and licking it like a child with a lollipop.

Max gently reached down and lifted her back up to her feet. He then began his own onslaught of licks and kisses over the upper half of her body. Josie began to feel almost faint with desire. She was soaking wet and afraid that if he carried on much longer she'd drown in her own juices.

He then pulled her onto the floor. Max began tracing outlines with his fingers over her body, teasing her by avoiding the one area where she needed to be touched.

Max moved his body over hers and headed on the journey south of Josie's navel. He kissed her knees, up the inside of her thighs, her hip bones, the mound of her pussy outside her panties and then back to her knees.

"Please," begged Josie," don't tease me any more, please."

Max gently eased off her lacy pants and ran the tip of his tongue along the length of her swollen clitoris. Josie hit the roof, with one of the fastest orgasms she had ever had in her life. It was short and sharp but very satisfying and Max wasn't stopping there. He continued to lick and kiss and bite and probe until Josie came again, this time a longer, slower very intense orgasm. She was soaking.

"You taste wonderful," said Max as he kissed her full on the mouth.

Josie ached to feel him deep inside her and told him so.

"Patience, patience," he replied, continuing with a slow, gentle massage of her breasts.

But by now Max couldn't wait either. He rolled onto his back and pulled Josie on top of him. She sat astride his hips and he slipped easily inside her. The feeling was unbelievable. He filled every part of her and it felt so good. Josie began moving up and down, left to right in perfect rhythm.

She then stretched out her legs and lay the length of him, her legs on his, her groin pushing against his hard, flat belly, picking up rhythm and speed until she could feel another orgasm approaching. "I'm coming again," she shouted as the orgasm hit with even more intensity than the last.

"Good for you," laughed Max who kept the sensation going for her for longer by pushing himself hard and deep inside her.

Josie was trembling. Max rolled her over and with his hips and thighs pressed down hard against hers, began thrusting deep and hard into her.

Josie came again and then felt Max orgasm. He pulled out of her and came in spurts over her stomach.

"Sorry," he said, "I didn't think to ask if you were on the pill or anything,"

Josie was grateful for his concern, though she was on the pill, just in case. Max got up to fetch some tissues. He gently wiped Josie's stomach and then lifted her up and took her into his bedroom.

Lying in his arms on his king size double bed, Josie couldn't believe what had just happened. She'd only known this man a few hours and here she was in his bed, in his flat, having the best sex ever.

She glanced at the clock, it was past 8.00 pm and they'd left Longchamps before 6.00 pm. Max saw her look.

"Do you have to get back?" he asked.

"Well, I've work in the morning and Chrissie has no idea where I am," she replied.

"I have to go to work too and you're only a few Métro stops away, "said Max. "You could be home in a few minutes in the morning. I'll make sure you get up early. Call your friend and tell her that you're staying over."

Josie couldn't resist the offer. She phoned her flatmate who seemed to be having a party of her own and wasn't the slightest bit concerned about her whereabouts, though Chrissie did seem a bit surprised to discover she was staying over with Max.

"Be careful Jose," said Chrissie, "Let's catch up tomorrow'"

After a quick shower, Max ran Josie a bath, gave her his dressing gown to wear and then made them both a delicious croque monsieur, swilled down with some ice cold beer.

They sat comfortably on his sofa, listening to music and chatting about their respective jobs and how they came to be living in Paris.

"Josie," said Max, "You really are something else, you know that!"

Josie smiled.

"But there's something I need to tell you."

Here we go thought Josie and braced herself for the 'I don't want commitment' line.

"I have a girlfriend," he continued rapidly. "We've been together two years now. We don't live together but she does stay here quite often. I'm sorry I didn't say anything before but I was completely swept away by you. I hope you don't think I'm an absolute bastard?"

Josie was quiet. She wasn't completely shocked, as this had all been too good to be true. Guys like this one didn't remain single for long.

"There aren't any traces of her here," replied Josie sharply, "did you plan a seduction for today then?"

"No, not at all," replied Max, "Anna, that's my girlfriend, is a bit of a fanatic when it comes to clutter. Everything must be in its place. You are OK about this aren't you Josie?"

Josie knew that her response would determine any possible future with Max. She could rant and rave and storm out or she could be really cool and see how things panned out. Girlfriends can be dumped can't they!

"Look Max," she said, lying through her teeth, "I had a good time and so did you. That's fine by me. I wasn't looking for a relationship so it's cool. Honestly."

Max whooped and hugged her tight.

"You really are great Josie," he said, "So understanding."

"And a bloody good actress," thought Josie putting on what she hoped was a sincere smile.

"Come on, "said Max, grabbing her hand and pulling her off the sofa.

And so another extraordinarily sensual session followed. Max, with one orgasm under his belt, had this stunning trick of bringing himself to the edge and then stopping, giving Josie what turned into hours of absolute pleasure.

They fell asleep with limbs around each other, "completely fucked," were the words that sprang to Josie's mind.

She slept for a few hours, waking early and just lay there thinking about the night before and how bitterly disappointed she really was to find out Max had a long standing, serious girlfriend.

"It sounds like he's right under her thumb, so if I have any chance with him I have to be the complete opposite - Fancy free!"

Josie had dozed back off to sleep by the time Max's alarm went off. He had set it extra early and immediately tucked his body in tightly against her back. He began caressing her breasts and between her legs and then took her quickly and sharply from that position, all the time manipulating her clitoris so that once again Josie experienced a soaring orgasm.

They showered together, soaping each other playfully. Josie was glad Max didn't try to have sex again she could hardly walk as it was.

She left the flat ahead of him and he said he'd call her that week. On the tube journey home Josie felt totally deflated.

Ellis Rose

CHAPTER 2

"That's what it will be like," she mused. "The ball in his court and me waiting for him to call when he can snatch a moment. Do I really want this?"

Putting these thoughts out of her mind, she climbed the stairs to the 5th floor flat and let herself in. Chrissie was still in bed so she took her a cup of tea and sat on the edge of the bed to tell her the news.

"That's what I meant by be careful," said Chrissie when Josie had finished her blow by blow account of the previous 12 hours. "Daniel told me Max has a girlfriend, bit of a dragon by the sound of it, very possessive and bossy too, apparently. Barely lets him out of her sight. Are you seeing him again?"

"I don't know," replied Josie. "He's absolutely gorgeous and the sex was phenomenal but I'm not sure I want to mope around waiting for him to phone when he fancies a bit on the side."

"Don't mope around then," said Chrissie. "Have a good time and if he calls, see him if you want to and don't if you don't. You can use him as much as he can use you."

"I have a great flatmate," shouted Josie jumping up from Chrissie's bed and giving her a hug.

Max did phone Josie later that week and they arranged for her to go around to his apartment the following Monday. "I've said I'm going football training," he explained, "And Anna plays tennis with the girls on a Monday so we should have plenty of chances to get together."

Josie was still unsure about this arrangement, but decided to take her friends' advice and go with the flow. The 'meetings' in Max's flat had been going on since then and although the sex was still good, Josie was becoming more and more convinced that there was no way of making Max split from Anna.

"Josie, Josie, for goodness sake," whined Angie. "Come back from wherever your mind's gone and let's order, I'm starving."

"OK, OK," she replied, "Sorry."

The food as usual was excellent at the Vieil Ecu but Angie obviously couldn't wait to get to the New Year's Eve party and insisted on them getting the bill as soon as they'd finished the main course.

Josie had opted for a goat's cheese salad with tomatoes followed by chicken in white wine sauce which was light but delicious. Daniel, predictably, had French onion soup and steak while Angie chose the most expensive items on the menu, oysters followed by lobster. She barely ate a mouthful of each, making Josie feel like a real porker having cleaned the plate of both courses, mopping up the dressing and sauce with several pieces of bread.

Daniel picked up the tab - wanting to impress Angie with his generosity no doubt thought Josie. She was embarrassed that Angie made no attempt to offer to pay for her share of the meal, even more so as she had picked such an expensive meal.

By 10 pm they had arrived at the club and the party was just about getting underway. Normally, the main function room was pretty bland with cream walls and faded dark red curtains and upholstery. Tonight though, the social committee had done themselves proud. There were panels of silver floating tails of foil covering the curtains; the battered and stained tables were hidden by bright red paper table cloths and decorated with silver candles and confetti style stars. Someone had had the foresight to attach a glitter ball to the ceiling in the middle of the dance floor and the strobe lights from the DJ's set, created a magical rainbow effect across the silver covered windows.

A few couples were dancing and the bar was packed. They found a table and Daniel went to get drinks. "Right, who's who and who's available?" asked Angie. "You'll have to ask Daniel that," Josie replied sharply, "I only know a few people here, they're more his crowd than mine."

When he returned with their drinks, Daniel took Angie around the room and introduced her to his friends. Josie stayed at the table, nursing her drink and keeping an eye on the door for a sighting of Max. She wasn't disappointed. Within a few minutes he arrived with not one, but two women on his arms: Anna and her best friend Jane.

From the first time she clapped eyes on her, Josie couldn't understand what Max saw in Anna. She had frizzy, mousy hair which wasn't cut in a particularly good style, small, 'piggy' eyes and no boobs at all. Max was always commenting about Josie's voluptuous bosom – no wonder she thought. Her friend Jane on the other hand was stunning: a tall willowy red head with sparkling green eyes and a wicked sense of humour. Even though she had only met her once, Josie liked Jane. She suspected Max quite liked Jane too from the way he talked about her.

Josie had only ever spoken with Anna once when she and Daniel had paired up for a mixed doubles tennis tournament held at the club back in the summer. In the semi-finals, Josie, who was a good tennis player, and Daniel who just used brute strength in his serve, found themselves playing against Max and Anna. Josie was determined to win and Max was equally keen to show off his skills. As a result, the match was very intense. Anna of course was totally oblivious to the competition between her boyfriend and their female opponent.

Josie and Daniel won in the end, after a hard fought match. Anna congratulated Josie on her game and asked her if she would like to join the girls at their regular Monday evening tennis sessions. Josie avoided catching Max's eye when she thanked Anna for the invitation but declined the offer, explaining that she couldn't make the commitment due to pressure of work. When they met the following Monday, Max teased her endlessly about her lame excuse. She pretended to laugh with him but in her heart of hearts, Josie couldn't help but feel used by him yet again. She also felt guilty about Anna.

"Goodness knows why", she thought to herself, "it's Max who should feel guilty, not me."

As the threesome of Max, Anna and Jane made their way across the room. Josie tried to look as nonchalant as possible and began a conversation with the people on the next table. But the music was too loud for chit chat. Fortunately, Daniel and Angie soon came back with Paul a friend of Daniel's whom Josie had met a few times before. He asked Josie if she wanted to dance and she accepted gladly.

Paul was very tall and slender with dark blue eyes and blond hair that fell over his forehead a bit like Huw Grant in his early films. Apparently he was an excellent cricketer and he did come over as a bit of a typical, public school type.

Josie suspected that Paul fancied her and so flirted with him blatantly, all for the sake of Max of course.

They'd been there for more than an hour before Max had a chance to speak to Josie as she emerged from the ladies loo.

"Hi gorgeous," he said, "You're looking great".

Josie knew she was looking good. She'd had her hair cut and blow dried that day and was wearing a new outfit – figure hugging black trousers and low cut white top which showed off her ample cleavage. Josie wasn't tall and slim, but she had a good figure and often drew admiring looks and comments from men. She had short, well cut, golden brown hair and huge dark brown eyes. "Come to bed eyes," many an ex had commented.

"You're not looking so bad yourself," she replied smiling, keeping the tone flippant. "Having a good time?"

"Better if I was back at the flat with you," he said quietly. "I've been watching you dancing. You really are very sexy."

Josie smiled, she'd been strutting her stuff all evening and was, in fact, having a good time. She'd left Daniel and Angie to their own devices and danced with Paul a few times as well as with several of his friends.

"Meet me downstairs in the ladies' changing rooms in ten minutes," said Max, his blue eyes burning brightly with hidden meaning. "I've got to have you here, tonight."

Josie was about to protest when Anna interrupted them. "That's where you are," she said, slipping a possessive arm through Max's and looking Josie up and down as if she had washed in off the street. "Come along darling, I want you meet Jane's new boyfriend."

"You remember Josie, don't you," Max said to Anna, obviously uncomfortable in the joint company of his girlfriend and lover.

"Of course I do, Max," she responded sharply. "I still haven't forgiven her for not joining our tennis group on a Monday. We need some challenging players, even if they aren't proper members of the club."

Josie remained silent. She was in fact enjoying Max's discomfort and really didn't care about Anna's comment about becoming a member. Every time she and Chrissie visited the Meudon club with Daniel, one member of the social committee tried to get them to part with their hard earned cash and pay a membership fee. Neither of the girls had the slightest intention of joining, particularly when they could get away with coming along when it suited them with Daniel.

She knew that, compared to Anna, who was wearing a very frumpy and boring plain black wool dress that emphasised her lack of boobs and lanky shape, she looked very sexy and glamorous.

"Sorry Anna," she said, "looking straight at Max. "But I have a regular appointment myself each Monday evening so it's still a 'no' I'm afraid."

Max went an even deeper shade of red and literally hustled Anna off in the direction of Jane and her new boyfriend. As they walked away, he turned to look over his shoulder at Josie. "Ten minutes," he mouthed, winking at her, confident that she would do exactly as he wanted.

Josie headed for the loo. She desperately wanted Max but an ultra quick shag in the ladies was so demeaning. "I'm not going to do it" she said to her reflection in the mirror.

"Talking to yourself now you mad cow!"

Angie emerged from one of the cubicles, eyes firmly on her own reflection in the mirror.

"Hi Angie, didn't realise you were there."

"Obviously, now come on let's go and get Daniel to buy us another drink. He may not be much to look at but he really is very sweet," said Angie dragging Josie out through the door.

"And so very rich too," thought Josie, "and that's the appeal no doubt."

They found Daniel chatting to Paul and some other friends and Paul asked Josie to dance again. She accepted knowing this would be the excuse not to meet Max downstairs.

A good half hour passed before Josie saw Max reappear. He was immediately accosted by Anna and they seemed to be having a bit of a row. "I'm not surprised," thought Josie, "she must have been wondering where he was."

It was soon midnight and once the clock struck 12.00, there was a lot of kissing and hugging among everyone there. Josie managed to avoid Max by concentrating on Paul, who was obviously delighted at the attention. She also noticed that Angie, unable to snare any other poor, unsuspecting male that evening, was snogging the face off Daniel as if her life depended on it.

When they eventually came up for air, Josie approached them and asked what time they were planning on leaving. She didn't really want to hang around trying to avoid Max for the rest of the evening. She also felt a bit guilty about leading Paul on.

"Oh, it's still all going on," replied Angie happily, indicating to Daniel that she needed another drink.

"Steady on a bit Ange," said Josie when Daniel had gone to the bar. "You're pretty slaughtered already."

"Don't be such a bore," slurred Angie. "Anyway you seem to have pulled with Paul, just enjoy yourself Josie and lighten up."

Josie spent the next few hours, warding off Paul's advances, avoiding eye contact with Max and basically having a pretty miserable time. At 2.00 am people finally started to leave.

"Would you like to come back to my place," Paul asked Josie as he helped her on with her coat.

"Oh Paul, that's kind of you," replied Josie, knowing full well that kindness wasn't on his mind. "But I can't really leave Angie, it's not fair."

Paul reluctantly agreed and asked if he could call next week to meet for lunch. Josie said yes of course and set off to find Daniel and Angie. They were already in Daniel's car about to set off.

"Hey, hold on," shouted Josie as the car started up.

"Sorry Josie," said Daniel, "Angie thought you may be going home with Paul so she's coming back with me to my place."

Josie looked at Angie. She was paralytic, slumped down in the car seat, skirt right up her backside and a glass of champagne in her hands.

"Don't spoil the party," she slurred, come and join us.

Josie had no choice as she had no means of getting back into Paris at this time of the morning. All of a sudden Paul's offer seemed preferable to playing gooseberry with Angie and Daniel. But Paul had already gone so Josie jumped in the back of the car hoping for the best. She'd had quite a lot to drink herself but wasn't anywhere near as drunk as Angie. Daniel, who was driving, was pretty sober though probably still well over the limit.

It was just a short drive to Daniel's house and by the time they arrived Angie was out for the count. Between them Josie and Daniel managed to get her into the house and eventually onto Daniel's very large, double bed. Josie indicated to Daniel to leave the room. She undressed Angie, pulling the duvet around her.

Daniel's was a white stoned, two bedroom farmhouse in lovely grounds just on the outskirts of Paris. There was a large open plan living/dining room with a real coal fire and stone walls, leading into a typical farm house style kitchen with a lovely warm Aga cooker and huge, untreated oak table.

Daniel had put the kettle on and was making a pot of coffee. "Just what the doctor ordered, I think," he said as Josie came into the kitchen.

"Thanks, Dan," she replied, "Listen, Angie is so drunk, I think I'd better sleep with her tonight in case she's sick or something and chokes."

She noted the disappointment on Daniel's face but knew he was essentially a good guy and wouldn't protest.

"Sure, I'll sleep in the spare room," he said, rather dejectedly.

"Look Dan," continued Josie, "I know Angie is fun, but she's a real man eater and you're far too nice for her. So have fun but don't get too smitten."

"Don't worry about me Jose, I can tell what Angie's like but you can't blame a chap for trying. At least it's a bit of fun, better than being on my own all the time."

Josie hadn't realised that Daniel was so very lonely, though she should have suspected by the way he bent over backwards to spend time and do anything for Chrissie.

"You are a nice guy," replied Josie, giving him a peck on the cheek. "I'm off to bed then. See you in the morning – or will it be afternoon."

Josie was so tired she just took off her boots and trousers and snuggled under the quilt next to Angie who was stark naked and snoring her head off. "She'd be mortified if Daniel or any other man come to that could hear her now," thought Josie letting the effects of the alcohol help her drift off to sleep.

It seemed that she had only been asleep for a short while when she was woken by the sounds of people talking. The bed felt rather crowded and she soon realised that Daniel was in the bed too – in the middle – whispering and giggling with Angie.

"Shit," thought Josie, "I hope they don't start to have it off while I'm in here with them. And I hope they don't think I'm going to join in."

She didn't know what to do. She could feign sleep and let them get on with it or she could get up and leave the bedroom. The first option was too unbearable to think about, the second would be so embarrassing.

"How the hell did I get myself into this situation," she thought to herself.

It was obvious that Daniel was trying to get it on with Angie who was still so plastered that she didn't have a clue what was going on. Eventually Daniel gave up and within a few minutes was snoring merrily away in his sleep.

Josie just lay there, still not sure whether to get up and risk waking the others. Eventually she fell asleep, only to be woken by Daniel turning over in his sleep and putting his hand on her breast.

"Three in a bed. No way," said Josie to herself, moving as far to the side of the bed as possible away from Daniel. She then very slowly, slid one leg and then the other out of bed and tip toed out of the bedroom.

Clad only in her bra, pants and 'party top', she went into the spare bedroom, grabbed the quilt from the spare bed, wrapping it around herself and snuggled down on the sofa in the sitting room. She checked the time, it was 7.30 am on New Year's day and here she was stuck in a house in the countryside, with a rampant couple and no means of escape.

She dozed for a while but couldn't settle so made herself a cup of coffee, found some bread, butter and jam and settled herself back on the sofa, not knowing how long she'd have to wait until the others emerged and they could leave. She had no intention of disturbing them.

The sofa was comfortable and she dozed on and off throughout the morning, half watching an inane French TV quiz programme, flicking between this and CNN news, half listening out for signs of life from the bedroom.

It was past midday when Angie and Daniel finally emerged. Josie offered them coffee and juice, glad to escape to the kitchen and away from their guilty looks. Angie followed her.

"Hi Jose, sorry I got so pissed last night. Don't remember

anything after midnight. Hope I wasn't too much trouble," said Angie with a pathetic look on her face.

"Maybe she doesn't realise I was in the bed too," thought Josie. "Well maybe she doesn't but Daniel certainly does, and he looks bloody guilty."

Josie and Angie took the juice and coffee into the sitting room. Daniel couldn't look Josie in the eye. "Serves you right," thought Josie. The three sat uncomfortably drinking coffee and making small talk until Josie said that really they ought to be getting back as she had a lot to do before going back to work the next day.

"Daniel has offered to take me to the airport tomorrow," said Angie. "So if you don't mind when we drop you off, I'll pick up my stuff and come back here. Save getting in your way in the morning."

Josie didn't know if she was pleased or disappointed. On the one hand she wouldn't have to listen to graphic details of Angie and Daniel's exploits; on the other hand she didn't really fancy spending the rest of the day on her own. Basically she had little choice in the matter.

Daniel dropped them off at the flat and waited in the car while Angie went up to collect her belongings. Josie sat in the living room with her coat still on, waiting for Angie to finish packing. They didn't speak at all.

When she'd packed all her stuff, Angie stuck her head around the living room door and said, "Cheers Josie, you're a pal. I'll give you a call when I get back tomorrow. Bye!"

"And thanks for nothing," thought Josie, feeling very sorry for herself. The flat felt cold and unlived in as both girls had been away for Christmas and Josie had only been back for a day before Angie arrived for the New Year. Chrissie was due back the next day – 2nd January – so she roused herself from the sofa, put the heating on, made herself a cup of coffee and began cleaning up the flat.

It was a typical Parisian flat with wood floors and high ceilings. There was a large entrance hall with storage cupboards for coats, two bedrooms, a large living/dining room with a balcony that overlooked the boulevard, a small kitchen and bathroom (with a tiny bench-bath) plus separate loo. The decor had originally been very dark and old fashioned but their landlady had given the girls the go-ahead to re-decorate, provided they didn't go mad. They had spent a day out at the Marché aux Puces at Port de Clingnancourt picking up bargain paint and had invited their friends, including Daniel, over to help paint the walls.

The apartment was now painted throughout in a pale cafe crème colour with loads of throws, rugs and scatter cushions in the sitting room and bedrooms, and a much lighter and brighter place to live.

Due to the wooden floors and dark wooden furniture, the flat did tend to get dusty. So Josie set to work with her duster and broom and soon the place was looking fresher at least. She put all her washing in a laundry bag ready for the morning. The laundry was conveniently situated just across the road and it only cost a few Euros for a big bag load of clothes or linen. Josie didn't really like the idea of the creepy man who worked in the laundry handling her clothes, especially her undies, but she had no choice. The flat wasn't big enough for a washing machine even if they could afford one.

Chores over, Josie went out onto the balcony which led off from the bedrooms. It was a glorious fine, cold but crisp winter's day and as she looked down the length of the street - rue de Rome - she wished she had someone to share it with.

"That's it," she said to herself, "No more mooning over Max. It's over. I'm going to get on with my life."

She decided to take herself off for a walk to the delicatessen a few streets away. It was open 24/7 and she'd be able to pick up something for her supper, some milk and maybe a bottle of wine too (now that her hangover from the night before had more or less gone).

Walking back up the five flights to the flat, their neighbours, the Beaudoin's, were coming down the stairs. Mother, father, son and daughter.

"Bonjour, Josephine," said Madame Beaudoin, "Bonne année, comment ça va?"

"Bonne année, bonne année, ça va bien merci," she replied.

The girls had a very up and down relationship with their neighbours, due principally to disagreements about noise levels and appropriate bed times. The flat mates' lifestyle didn't really appeal to Madame Beaudoin. Monsieur and young master Beaudoin however didn't seem to mind the girls at all.

This all changed though when Josie and Chrissie offered the

daughter, Isabelle, English lessons for free. These were taken in the Beaudoin household so Mrs Beaudoin could keep an eye on things and make sure the English girls didn't lead young Isabelle astray. The lessons were lively and fun and usually ended with Monsieur Beaudoin opening a bottle of wine to share - and more often than not one bottle led to a few more.

The lessons had lapsed during the build up to Christmas and the holiday period so Josie told Isabelle on the stairwell that they'd be happy to start up again in the New Year. Isabelle seemed pleased though her mother didn't look quite so happy when she saw her husband's eyes light up.

"It's been very quiet without you girls here," she said to Josie. Josie didn't miss the meaning. They'd had a few friends around before Christmas but the few turned into 20-odd and they had ended up doing the conga down in the street in the early hours.

"Oh don't worry," replied Josie wickedly, "Chrissie is back tomorrow – I can't wait to get back to our usual routines."

Madame Beaudoin frowned and continued down the stairs. Monsieur Beaudoin winked at Josie and she couldn't help but wink back. "Poor sod," she thought as she let herself into the flat, "totally hen pecked."

Ellis Rose

CHAPTER 3

She unpacked her shopping, had a long soak in the bath, made herself some bread and cheese, opened a bottle of red wine and settled in front of the TV. She must have dozed off as she was woken by the phone ringing. As she jumped up, she knocked the wine off the side table and it spilt all over her. "Shit," she said as she picked up the receiver.

"Shit? That's no greeting for a lonely, horny man on this joyful New Year's Day. How are you gorgeous?"

It was Max. Josie was dumbstruck – he was the last person she expected to hear from.

"Josie, are you there? Josie?"

"Sorry Max," she replied, finally able to speak. "I just spilled a glass of wine all over myself."

"I'll come and lick it off, if you like."

"Funny ha, ha," said Josie, "and how exactly are you going to manage that?"

"I can be over at your place within 10 minutes," he replied. "Chrissie is still away isn't she?"

"Yes, she's due back tomorrow."

"See you in a few minutes then," said Max and hung up.

"Bugger," thought Josie as she caught a glimpse of her appearance in the hall mirror. "I look like shit."

Ignoring the red wine spill she hurled herself into the bedroom. Stripped of the baggy joggers and jumper she had been wearing. Unable to find any 'sexy' undies of her own, she rummaged through Chrissie's draw and found a pretty, lacy thong which was nearly the same colour as her new pink bra. "No time to dress," she thought, "and thank goodness I had a bath earlier. I'll wear my new silk dressing gown and get some slap on instead of clothes."

By the time Max was ringing the intercom, Josie felt just about presentable. She used a towel to mop up the spilled wine and chucked it in the laundry bag just as he knocked on the apartment door.

Josie's heart was beating fast as she let Max into the flat. This was the first time he had come here and she was a bit embarrassed that their flat was not quite the pristine palace he lived in.

Max looked great and all the resolve about not seeing him again disappeared the second she caught sight of him. He was wearing jeans, loafers and sweatshirt with nothing underneath. His hair was damp from the shower and he had a slight unshaven look which suited some men but not all – it definitely suited Max.

"Good of you to dress for the occasion," he said laughing as he handed her a carrier bag from the same deli she had visited a few hours earlier.

"Well, you didn't give me much time, did you," Josie replied checking out the contents of the bag which included two bottles of champagne and a huge punnet of strawberries.

"Food for lovers," said Max quietly as he took the bag out of Josie's hands and kissed her hard on the mouth.

Josie couldn't resist him and her body, with a will of its own, responded eagerly. With an urgency Josie hadn't felt with Max since the first time in his flat, she pulled him tightly to her, feeling the urgency of his erection against her leg.

Max undid her dressing gown and slid it off her shoulders. Kissing her neck, her shoulders, the top of her breasts, he removed her bra and then the thong roughly, ripping some of the lace. Then with his mouth still on hers he undid his trousers releasing his erection.

He lifted Josie up against the front door and thrust himself deep inside her. Josie wrapped her legs around his waist and he pushed himself even deeper. They came together in a quick but intense orgasm that left Josie's head reeling.

"Josephine, Josephine, tout va bien?" exclaimed a voice from outside the door. It was Madame Beaudoin. The family had been returning home and the sounds coming from Josie's hallway had caused them concern.

"Oui, oui, I'm fine," Josie replied. "Just doing a bit of exercise, sorry to have disturbed you."

Josie and Max burst into fits of laughter as they extricated themselves from one another. "Best exercise in the world," said Max pulling his jeans up.

"Bathroom's just down the corridor," indicated Josie. "The towels are all clean."

She quickly retrieved Chrissie's borrowed underwear and her dressing gown and noticed the torn thong. "Shit, what will Chrissie say?" she said to herself. "I'll deal with that later, I'll just have to go knickerless for now, there's nothing clean and matching."

Josie always wore matching underwear, she had 'a thing' about it – it made her feel good.

Max was already in the sitting room when Josie went in with the carrier bag of goodies. They shared some bread and cheese and then opened a bottle of champagne which they polished off with the strawberries.

They talked easily about safe subjects. Josie didn't dare ask where Anna was and Max didn't mention the missed opportunity of the night before. "We're just playing games," thought Josie to herself, listening to Max talk about his job and possible promotion.

"Why do I let this guy do this to me? It's not just the sex. There's a spark between us, why can't he see it. Well, I'm going to make him see it." These were her thoughts as she put down her champagne glass and moved across the sofa to sit astride Max.

Now it was her turn. She covered his face, his eyelids, the corners of his mouth, his neck, everywhere with soft, butterfly kisses whilst at the same time gently moving her groin over his. She stood up, removed her dressing gown and sat astride him again, holding his shoulders back against the sofa so he couldn't touch her easily. She lifted off his sweatshirt and undid his jeans. Falling to her knees in front of him, she removed his shoes, socks, trousers and pants and began caressing him from that position.

After a few moments of manipulation, he was rock hard again. Josie held his penis like it was some treasured object and began licking the length of it, flicking her tongue over the tip and down to his balls. His groans indicated that he wanted more. Josie took his shaft in her mouth, moving her lips up and down deeper and deeper, making sure she didn't hurt him with her teeth. Max was calling out her name, telling her she was wonderful, she was the best and Josie loved the power this gave her over him.

"He's all mine now," she said to herself, "I'll bet stuck up Anna doesn't do this for him."

Max had never been a selfish lover and feeling himself close to release he gently removed his penis from Josie's mouth and lifted her onto his lap again.

Wanting to make this last, Josie rubbed herself along his penis until her clitoris was swollen and throbbing. "That feels so good," said Max surprised. "For me too," replied Josie moving harder and faster until she came in a short, sharp burst wetting the length of him.

Turning around, she then sat on his lap with her back to him, guiding him deep inside her. "Touch me, please," she cried out as their mutual thrusting heightened, heading towards climax. Max began rubbing Josie's clitoris, searching for the swollen, red tip he knew would make her hit the ceiling. Josie came again and Max, desperate for release, pushed her to her feet and took her from behind, brutally but erotically. He slammed his penis deep inside her and shouted out with pleasure as he came.

As their breathing subsided Max put his arms around Josie, drawing her close to him. "That was sensational," he whispered gently in her ear. "You are one hell of a woman."

Josie was speechless from a mix of sex and the tenderness he was now showing her. She was desperate to say, "I'm all yours," but stopped herself as she knew Max would be turned off if she put any pressure on him at all.

She wasn't stupid just besotted. She was incredibly attracted to Max, more than any other man she had ever met. But she also realised that he was an out and out player. His behaviour on New Year's Eve confirmed this opinion but she still couldn't resist him. She knew, as she had that very first evening that they had slept together, that the only way to maintain his interest was to play it very cool indeed.

In the past, Josie had had her fair share of relationships from her school yard boyfriend to one night stands at University and a few foreign flings during her year spent in Switzerland. She had always been the one to end these relationships, not wanting to be tied down before realising her dream of living and working abroad.

But Max had hit a raw nerve and she had never felt this strongly about a man before.

She realised that part of the attraction was his 'unavailability' but she also recognised that if he was free for a full time, permanent relationship, she wouldn't say no.

"You're welcome to stay," she said, her tone light and non-committal.

"Try and stop me," he replied. "I've had too much champagne to drive home anyway. Can I grab a quick shower?"

While Max was showering, Josie put the dishes in the sink and then showered herself. By the time she was done Max was already in bed and drifting off to sleep. Snuggling up to him Josie wished with all her heart that it could be like this forever, or more often at least. She knew Max was using her, but had convinced herself that she was using him too. The big difference was that he had someone else in his life whilst she didn't.

"Just enjoy it while you can you stupid girl," she said to herself as she too drifted off to sleep. "It will all work out one day."

Ellis Rose

CHAPTER 4

When Josie woke the next morning Max was already up and dressed. "You forgot to set the alarm," he said sharply.

"Sorry, I'm usually pretty good at waking anyway. What time is it?"

"It's 7.30 already and I have to get home, showered, shaved and out again by 8.00. I've got an 8.30 meeting. And the traffic will be horrendous first day back after the holidays, Shit!"

Josie felt guilty even though it wasn't all her fault. "Sorry," she said again getting out of bed and reaching for her dressing gown.

"I'll call you," muttered Max as he searched his pockets for his car keys.

"On the phone table in the hall," she replied catching sight of her dishevelled image in the dressing table mirror.

"Cheers, see you."

And he was gone. Josie felt deflated and cheap. Not even a peck on the cheek. "You are going to have to get over him," she said to herself, "he's just using you." Yet as she remembered their love making of the night before, she felt the tell tale stirrings in her groin. "But it's so good, why can't I enjoy it for what it is and forget about the emotions."

It was her turn to rush as she started work at 8.30 am herself and though it wasn't far and her boss was pretty laid back, she had loads to do. She also wanted to leave on time and get some shopping in before Chrissie arrived home later that evening.

Josie worked in a small office near Place de la Concorde which was the European sales office of a large, American organisation called Chemfast which dealt in chemicals. Although Josie wasn't really clear what was involved in the technical side of things. There were only a handful of employees and she was PA to the European Chairman, Jean Carrère, known to everyone as JC. Her friend Libby, also English, was the accountant and office administrator and there were two older French ladies who dealt with orders and supplies.

Josie had only worked there for six months and was concerned that there was talk of moving the office to London as the Americans didn't really get on with the French and felt there would be less language problems if the office was in the UK. Josie had decided that if the office was moved she would stay in Paris and look for another job. She had studied so hard to have the chance of working abroad and she wasn't ready to go home yet.

Libby wasn't sure what she would do. She thought she may go to London short term to help set up the office but, like Josie, wasn't ready to move back to the UK permanently.

The girls had hit it off from day one. Josie had been offered the job at Chemfast, and Libby had got in touch straight away and arranged to meet up the weekend she arrived to help settle her in. They had met outside Notre Dame and after a few tentative minutes of introductions, Libby asked Josie what she wanted to do. They settled on a quick drink in one of the bars on the Boulevard St Michel. The quick drink turned into an afternoon's session and broke the ice immediately between the two young women.

There were some spooky similarities between them which they became aware of during their first conversation. They were the same age, with the same birthday and both had a degree in French. They both loved wine and had other similar interests like reading and tennis. Appearance wise they were very different though. While Josie was small, dark and voluptuous, Libby was tall, willowy and virtually flat chested. She commented on this during their first afternoon's conversation.

"You're so lucky, Josie," slurred Libby after their second bottle of wine. "Look at mine, pimples. A man walked past me the other day and said "oh, those poor little ones. When I'm rich and famous, I'm definitely going to have a boob job."

"Big boobs aren't all they're cracked out to be," replied Josie, slurring equally as badly as Libby. "I mean, mine look fine squashed into a platform bra with low cut top, but believe me, they're well on their journey south already and I'm only 23!"

They didn't get to see much of Paris that day but made up for it over the next few weeks with Libby acting as Josie's guide, principally of the bars, restaurants and cinemas and above all the fantastic apartment stores on the Boulevard Haussman and the quirky boutiques which they were forever discovering down all the little sides streets across the city.

Josie loved shoes and many a weekend she, Chrissie and Libby would wander the length of the city discovering new clothes and shoe shops at bargain prices. The last time she counted she had more than twenty pairs of court shoes, at least eight pairs of boots and that was without checking the sandals, flip flops and special occasion shoes. She dreamed of owning a pair of Jimmy Choos but these were way out of her price range. Her favourites were a pair of kitten heel, red sling backs that her mum had bought her the previous summer on a shopping trip to Bath. She had no clothes to match the shoes but loved them anyway and wore them around the flat like slippers, to break them in.

Chrissie and Libby were always teasing her about her shoe fetish but she didn't care... she loved them anyway.

Libby had her own flat in the 16th arrondissement. When she first arrived, the company had found Josie a room in a 'Foyer for 'Jeunes Travailleuses' – principally a hostel for French girls moving from the provinces into Paris to study or work. Josie hated it there. It was just like a university hall of residence with a cheap and cheerful canteen. Although Josie generally didn't eat in the canteen, on the few occasions that she did, she had been propositioned by one of the Tunisian kitchen helpers. So she was desperate to get out.

Josie had met a couple of English girls, both students on a tight budget, at the Foyer. One of them, Allie, was also looking for a flat as her boyfriend was due to join her shortly. She had tried everywhere but everything was too expensive. She passed one advert which she had found on the English Church notice board, onto Josie. It was a bit too expensive for Allie and anyway the advert was for a single female. And that's how Josie met Chrissie and moved into Rue de Rome.

Chrissie and a college friend Alex had originally moved over to Paris together. But Alex had a boyfriend back home and after 12 months of living away from him decided to move back. Chrissie was struggling with the rent on her own so put out an ad for a flatmate. Josie was the only person to respond. Naturally Chrissie didn't tell her that at first.

Josie was quite nervous when she arrived at Rue de Rome for a visit and interview. The flat was five flights up with no lift. "Shopping must be fun," she thought to herself as she rang the doorbell.

When Chrissie answered, Josie took in her appearance straight away - a slender brunette with dark brown eyes and friendly, open face. She showed Josie in and explained why she was looking for a flatmate. Chrissie then gave Josie the grand tour and explained that as last in she would have the smallest bedroom. Josie didn't mind. She was so desperate to get out of the Foyer that a cupboard would have done. Besides, the room was large enough and as it was next to the sitting room, it had a small balcony of its own overlooking the street. Also the location was perfect as it was only a short Métro ride or even walking distance on a fine day from her office on the Rue Royale.

As she stood on the sitting room balcony, looking out on the street, Josie really hoped that Chrissie would let her move in. It was a beautiful spring evening and the street was quiet at the end of the working day. "I do hope she'll say yes," thought Josie, "I can really see myself living here."

"Do you want time to think about it," Chrissie asked her once she'd shown her around and asked Josie a few questions about herself and her job. Josie didn't hesitate. "No, I'd really love to take it, if you'll have me," she replied.

"Well I have a few more people to see so I'll give you a call tomorrow evening and let you know," said Chrissie. Only later on did Josie find out that no-one else had answered the ad and that Chrissie didn't want to seem too eager in case she scared Josie away.

Josie was on tenterhooks for the next 24 hours as she loved the flat and had taken to Chrissie too. When Chrissie rang the next evening and told her the place was hers, she whooped for joy and thanked her profusely. She moved in the following weekend and for Chrissie her lifestyle in Paris was never the same again.

Josie was essentially a party animal. She had always enjoyed going out even as a young teenager with her gang of local friends. She always worked hard too – whether at school, college or now her career. But in her view, if you worked hard you deserved to party hard too – and have good clothes, shoes, and a great social life in general.

Chrissie had been a bit more subdued and Josie put this down to her previous boring flatmate. The first day Josie moved into the flat she had unpacked within half an hour and asked Chrissie if she had any plans. Josie had arranged to meet Libby and invited her new flatmate to join her. They met on the Champs Elysées. After going to see the latest cult French film about a man who was having an affair with his next door neighbour, they went to a bistro down one of the side streets which offered a set menu, and was well away from the expensive main tourist stretch.

Josie ordered wine as soon as they sat down and despite protests from Chrissie that she would have a soft drink, they persuaded her to have wine. Needless to say, the evening turned into a bit of a night and the girls ended up going home by taxi as they were too drunk to even contemplate the Métro.

The next day, Chrissie had a mega hangover but Josie was fine. "Never again," said Chrissie. But this was the start of many an evening out for the threesome.

Josie couldn't help but smile remembering her first evening with her new best friends, Chrissie and Libby. Checking her watch, she hurried out of the flat and out onto the street towards the Métro.

When Josie arrived at the office, 15 minutes late, her boss JC still hadn't turned up but Madame Vergne and Madame Pontilly were already at work. Though generally formal, they were very kind to Josie and Libby as each had children of their own and felt quite protective toward the two English girls living so far from home. Josie and Libby played up to them of course and the result was many a culinary treat as 'the girls probably weren't eating properly'.

Madame Vergne was also trying to get them to go to her church but the girls had managed to wheedle out of this by saying they belonged to a specific British religion that believed in the worship of that sacred bird, the Owl. The girls thought it was hysterical and would often make 'twooting' noises if they thought that Madame Vergne was listening to them.

After exchanging normal New Year niceties, Josie settled

down at her desk to check out her post and emails. There were lots from friends wishing her happy new year and she was so absorbed in these that she didn't hear JC come in and stand behind her.

"Bonne année Josie," he said, making her jump out of her seat. "Oh hello JC, bonne année," she replied quickly shutting down her email inbox so he couldn't see all her personal messages.

To be fair, JC was a good boss. He paid them well and always paid overtime if they stayed late to prepare for a conference or seminar. It was just that sometimes he was rather unpredictable. He could be the life and soul of the office, joking with them and distracting them from their work and the next minute chastising them for not getting everything done on time. He had been particularly difficult just before Christmas and the others had put it down to the possibility of the office moving from Paris to London.

JC's life was completely upside down. He had originally set up Chemfast's European Office several years before in London and so had moved his wife and children out there. It was JC who persuaded the Americans to move the office to Paris (more central to the rest of Europe was his reason). His real motive was his lovely, young mistress Muriel. As his children were still at school in the UK, his family stayed over there, while he spent most of his time in Paris. Everyone knew about this situation but it was never openly acknowledged, even though Muriel often came to the office to meet JC for lunch. Their lunchtime absences more often than not extended late into the afternoon with JC popping briefly back into the office to sign any mail or check his messages.

Moving the office back to London would ruin his idyllic lifestyle, so no wonder he had been grumpy. Today however he was full of the joys and Josie discovered later that he had been in Paris over the New Year without his wife and children.

Josie and Libby's office was straight off the main entrance. It was large, light and airy with big oak desks and comfortable leather computer chairs. The room also contained all the filing cabinets, photocopier, printers etc… though these were cordoned off by wall dividers. There was a waiting area with a couple of low seated sofas and a coffee table. Sometimes there was so much hectic bustle going on that the girls found it hard to concentrate. But at the same time Josie loved the 'buzz' of people to-ing and fro-ing. Libby would have preferred it to be a bit quieter.

The Madames shared a large but dark room at the back of the

building and JC's office (in which he seemed to spend very little time unless he was on the phone) was the smallest. All the rooms were decorated tastefully in creams and browns with good quality furniture and office equipment. Looking around JC sighed.

"Remind me, when is Libby back," he asked Josie, sitting at Libby's desk and draping his long, skinny legs over the side. "Not till Monday," she replied, "Remember it's her parents' wedding anniversary party this weekend."

Looking at him, Josie never failed to be amazed at the success JC had with women. He was tall and quite gangly, with thinning brownish hair, which looked like it had been touched up with some sort of male hair dye. He wore quite extraordinary un-coordinated clothes and very large glasses which hid a lot of his face. Libby thought he was very attractive in a 'French' sort of way but Josie couldn't see it herself and certainly couldn't see what a beauty like Muriel saw in him. "Hidden talents or money I guess," she thought to herself as she got up from her desk to pour him a cup of coffee from the machine which was always kept topped up, for JC more than anyone.

"Good, we need to have a staff meeting about the relocation of the office as soon as she gets back," he said.

"So it is going ahead then," asked Josie despondently.

"Looks like, you know what the Americans are like… once they decide something. Shame really, we'll never get offices like these in London."

"Actually JC, I think this is the best time to tell you that I won't be moving back to London. I've only been in Paris a short while and it's been my dream to live abroad, so I guess I'll have to start looking for another job. I'll do all I can to help with the move of course and would very much appreciate your advice on finding a new job."

Josie was relieved that JC now knew her plans and waited for his reaction. But JC was fine. "Sure Josie, I understand and I'd do the same in your position. Let's have the meeting all together on Monday when Libby's back and we can start planning accordingly then. This affects all of us of course. Madame Vergne and Madame Pontilly won't want to move. Do you know what Libby's plans are?"

"You'll have to ask her that," replied Josie not wishing to share her friend's confidences.

The rest of the day passed pretty quickly and JC didn't bother to come back to the office after lunch with Muriel. Josie also managed to leave early and pop to the supermarket on her way home. Back at the flat, she had a quick tidy up and prepared an easy supper of salad, meats, cheeses, baguette and, of course, some wine ready for when Chrissie got home.

She'd only just stepped out of the shower when she heard a key in the door. "I'm back," Chrissie shouted from the hallway, gladly dropping her bags and cases after climbing up five flights of stairs. Josie ran out to the hallway and gave her flatmate a big hug, losing her towel in the process.

"Too much bare flesh," laughed Chrissie returning Josie's hug. "So how has it been? How was your New Year's Eve?"

"I'll tell you over supper, which is ready when you are. It's so good to have you back, especially after having Angie to stay for a few days."

Once Chrissie had unpacked, they sat down to supper and Josie filled her in on Angie and Daniel's New Year's antics. She found it really funny, especially the three in the bed episode. Josie of course didn't tell her about Max but Chrissie knew he would have been at the New Year's do.

"So did you see the lovely Max at the party then," she asked.

"Of course, he was with the delightful Anna. Actually I spent most of the evening dancing and chatting with Paul and he's going to call me next week for lunch. In fact, if Angie hadn't been so drunk, I was going to have a lift home with Paul. But I was really worried about her… or Daniel… I'm not sure which really."

"So what's happening with Max then, Josie? Any New Year's resolutions you want to tell me about?"

"Not really, just see what happens. I'm not going back to the way things were though – no way."

"Good," said Chrissie and she meant it although she was unsure if Josie did.

Josie explained about the office moving back to London and Chrissie said she would ask at her company if there was anything going. "But I want to be more than just a secretary," thought Josie. "I want to do something a bit different so will start looking from tomorrow, no point in waiting until the last minute."

"So what do you fancy doing? You must have given it some thought?" Josie looked lost in contemplation and Chrissie couldn't help but laugh. "Have you thought about becoming a relationship advisor?" said Chrissie, tongue firmly in cheek. "Or of course you could consider a long term position as a shoe-shopaholic'.

Josie stuck one, un-ladylike finger up at her flat mate.

"Ha, ha," she said. "You're only jealous, I mean look at your 'clophes'... she used the jargon that her French colleagues used at the office. "My gran wouldn't be seen dead in those."

It was Chrissie's turn to make a rude gesture. "Comfort over fashion, Jose. Well at least in the sanctuary of our flat."

Banter over the girls had an early night as they both had work the next day, though it was a short week due to the New Year's break. On Saturday morning they slept late, waking up to an enchanting snow that covered Paris. They decided to go for a walk to their favourite bar on the Ile St Louis, le Café de la Paix (known to the Brits as the Oasis). The walk took them down past the Gare St Lazare, onto Boulevard Haussman past all the big department stores, down Rue Royal to Place de la Concorde and onto the rue du Faubourg St Honoré and then past the Hotel Intercontinental on rue Scribe and across the Seine into the Latin Quarter.

Josie loved the fact that Paris was so compact you could basically walk around it in a day. The walk from their flat to the Latin quarter took around 45 minutes despite the snow and the girls were ready for a hot chocolate.

The Oasis was a favourite haunt of the English people living in Paris but on this particular day it was pretty quiet. It was a traditional Parisian Bistro where all the waiters wore long white aprons over their white shirts and black trousers. The front of the premises was the bar area made up of a large counter with a massive, gleaming coffee machine dominating. A few dark mahogany tables and chairs were placed next to the windows but mainly people tended to stand up and lean on the massive bar counter.

The restaurant was through an archway and was crammed with oblong tables adorned with red and white checked cloths. Many a time the girls had found themselves sitting next to interesting strangers over a traditional meal of steak, frites and bottle of red wine.

The first time Josie went with Chrissie and Libby to the Oasis she literally felt that she was a true Parisian citizen. From the decor, ambience and the way the waiters were dressed in their black trousers and shirts and long white aprons, the restaurant was like something out of a traditional French film.

They stayed in the bar for around 30 minutes before taking the Métro home. They spent the evening chatting and listening to music. This was the sort of evening Josie needed after the excitement of the New Year. They spent Sunday relaxing and just pottering around.

That Sunday evening Libby phoned to say she was back and to check what had been happening. Josie decided to save the Angie/Daniel saga until the next day but told Libby about the meeting regarding the office move. "Not surprising really," she replied. "How does JC feel about it?"

"Seemed OK, I'll bet he's got something up his sleeve though. I can't see him giving up his current lifestyle that easily."

At work the next day, JC called the team together and outlined the plans for the office move. The aim was to get everything ready by March so they could move at the end of the month and be established by the end of the financial year.

Libby agreed to work with JC on the move and set up the office in London, provided she was able to maintain her apartment in Paris. She had every intention of moving back once they found someone to replace her. Both the Madames confirmed they would not be moving to London and would look around for new employment. Unlike Josie, neither of them actually needed to work, and so were very relaxed about the whole situation.

But Josie had a gnawing ache at the pit of her stomach at the end of the meeting. She definitely didn't want to go back to the UK but what if she couldn't find a new job. She knew she could always temp, like Chrissie had when she first moved to Paris, but she didn't really fancy that. Lunchtime she went out and bought the newspaper to check out the vacancies. There's wasn't much in there but JC reassured her that it was still early in the New Year as spring approached there would no doubt be more opportunities. He also assured her that if he heard of anything he would let her know.

The week passed really quickly with just a few months to complete the move, Josie and Libby had extra work on top of their usual day-to-day jobs. The following weekend Josie and her friends went on a shopping spree among the smaller boutiques they had discovered away from the expensive department stores and exclusive designer shops.

Josie found a stunning green wool dress which clung to her figure showing off all the good bits. This with a black jacket will be good for interviews she thought, as she paid for the dress. But the feelings of concern for her future prospects continued to prey on her mind as the girls carried on shopping. "Perhaps I should think about saving some money rather than spending it," she said to herself as she tagged along with the others, "just in case I can't find another job."

On Saturday evening the two flatmates and Libby went out to a popular bar on the Boulevard St Michel and then a jazz club, Le Caveau de la Huchette. It was one of those underground clubs, always packed, with the locals jiving to anything and everything.

The girls had been to the club several times and had really enjoyed the atmosphere and music. The first time they ventured down the steep steps into the club's darkness they felt very out of place, overdressed and tacky in their party clothes. They knew they stood out and hadn't stayed for long. Now they were hardened visitors, fitting in with the locals dressed in jeans and casual tops and accessories.

The regulars at Le Caveau de la Huchette were only interested in the music and dancing, very different from your standard British nightclub. Josie, Chrissie and Libby felt privileged that they were now wholly accepted in this amazingly cool environment which had become their favourite weekend haunt.

The drinks were expensive but the atmosphere fantastic and the music sensational. Famous jazz musicians often just turned up there to jam with the locals. The place wasn't as busy as usual so they managed to get a table.

"Here we are again," said Chrissie, "three stunning, women about town and not a man between us."

"I know," replied Libby, "I mean I'm not looking for the love of my life but a date now and again would be good."

The others laughed. "Well I've found the love of my life," said Josie, "but he's only interested in one thing and regular dating isn't it."

The others groaned. "Not Max again… Josie, you are not allowed to mention the 'M' word for the rest of the evening, promise," said Chrissie rolling her eyes.

"OK, I know I'm a bore about it but he's under my skin. I

promise not to mention him again," said Josie sheepishly.

She summoned the waiter to bring them another round of drinks. When he returned, the waiter indicated toward a group of young men standing at the bar. "These drinks have been paid for by some admirers," he said to them.

The girls turned towards the bar and were pleasantly surprised to see three, good looking guys dressed nearly identically in jeans, plain white t-shirts and leather jackets, smiling at them. The handsome guys sauntered over to the table and the tallest of the three, spoke first.

"We hope you aren't offended but it's not often we see such lovely ladies together in here, so we wondered if we could join you?"

They pulled up three chairs and sat at the girls' table. They introduced themselves and were funny and laconic. Claude was undoubtedly the most attractive with dark, olive skin, a mop of curly hair, sparkling brown eyes and the whitest teeth they had ever seen.

Christian was shorter than Claude with a less obviously Mediterranean look. He also had dark hair that was sleeked back off his smooth forehead and which emphasised his dark blue eyes. He also had a wide, warm mouth that sat naturally in a permanent smile.

The third guy, Yves, was the total opposite to his friends. Tall and fair with a strong Parisian accent, he was the city born 'dude' who had introduced his friends from the south of France to the most popular local venues.

The girls introduced themselves and it was only then the men realised they were English. They seemed delighted at the fact and the conversation flowed easily. They explained that they were all air traffic controllers working at Paris's second airport, Orly. At first the girls didn't believe them but they produced their security cards to prove it. They had come to the club straight from work, explaining that the concentration required of the job could be very stressful and so they needed to unwind.

They danced with the girls and were all excellent dancers, jiving to anything in true French style.

Claude seemed very taken with Chrissie and vice versa; whilst Josie and Christian also drifted towards each other. Yves tried to chat up Libby but she seemed a bit bored by him. Libby generally preferred older men and had recently come out of a difficult relationship with a married man.

At 2 a.m. the club was still lively but the girls were ready to leave.

"Let us take you home," offered Claude, "we have our car outside."

"What is it, a minibus," retorted Libby quickly. Her tone was a bit sharp but the men didn't seem to pick up on it.

"Thanks for the offer," said Chrissie "but we'll get a taxi."

The three guys looked very disappointed but in reality couldn't have fitted all three girls in their little Renault 5, not legally anyway.

Chrissie gave Claude and Christian the phone number of the flat and they promised to call the next day.

"Don't hold your breath," said Libby.

"What's up with you then," Josie asked her friend. "You were quite off with those guys and I thought they were lovely?"

"I don't know," replied Libby. "I just can't stop thinking about Matt at home. I saw him at Mum and Dad's party. It was really upsetting. The lovely Lia was there too, of course…Look Josie, I know we have a pop at you about Max but I really do understand you know. When a guy gets under your skin, he can be very hard to resist. Believe me, I've been there. I know how you feel."

Josie kept quiet. As they travelled back to the flat in the taxi, she looked out the window at the passing Parisian streets, remembering when Libby had confided in her about Matt and the passionate affair that made her want to leave England.

Libby's father was a vicar in a village in Berkshire and sounded quite strict by all accounts, treating Libby and her sisters like mini slaves at home. During her holidays from college, Libby acted as sort of unofficial nanny to the twin boys of one of their neighbours. Matt, the father was a surgeon and the mother, Lia was a very successful marketing director in London. For the three years before Libby came to Paris she had been sleeping with Matt on the many occasions when his wife was away and she was responsible for the twins.

Part of Libby's decision to come to work in Paris was to try to end the relationship with Matt but every time she went home, she just couldn't resist him. The previous summer, she and Matt had almost been caught by Lia. Since then Lia had treated Libby differently and was suspicious of leaving her alone with her husband. So when she went home at Christmas, Libby told Matt it was over with once and for all.

As Libby hopped out of the cab outside her flat, Josie followed her up to the front door. "Let's go for a drink after work on Monday, Lib and have a chat. I think we both need a shoulder to cry on."

"OK," replied Libby sadly. "You know what will happen though… we'll end up slaughtered, put the world to rights, re-invent mankind to suit our own needs and be totally incapable of work the next day… sounds great."

Once Josie was back in the cab, Chrissie asked her if everything was OK with Libby. "I think so. She's just a bit fed up with work and everything I think."

CHAPTER 5

Back at work on Monday, Josie double checked that Libby was still OK to go out for a drink that evening and then had to go out to deliver some photos to the studio which produced all the graphic displays they used for exhibitions and seminars. They had a big event coming up in Brussels which Josie had overall responsibility for and she really didn't want anything to go wrong this time.

The first event she had done for the company with JC had been a bit of a disaster as despite claiming she was experienced in exhibition work, she had never run one in her life! At the trade fair in Madrid, she had proudly unveiled the new exhibition stand which she had worked so hard on with the designers. Unfortunately, Josie hadn't had the foresight to check out the display before it was packed up and despatched to Spain. There was just one typo: the word 'Public' was missing the 'l'. JC was furious and Josie absolutely mortified. Fortunately, all the company's customers thought it was really funny and overnight Josie had gained a reputation for being 'quite a girl' - a reputation she wasn't sure she relished in the face of some of the older Spanish customers who seemed to think it was OK to paw her at any given moment.

Having triple checked the artwork for the invitation brochure for the Brussels exhibition, Josie returned to the office and checked her voicemail. The previous week she had applied for a couple of jobs and one message was from a company inviting her for an interview the following Thursday. "Great," she thought, "perhaps finding a new job won't be all that hard after all."

The second message was from Max. Josie's heart stopped beating and her hands started to shake. "Hi gorgeous," said Max in his usual sexy way, "Just checking we're on for tonight. Seems like ages since I've seen you. I can't wait. Give me a bell on my mobile to confirm."

Josie was in turmoil. She could ignore the message (which would be the sane, sensible thing to do) or she could go running around to his flat again like the silly woman she had been in the past, at his beck and call when it suited him. Despite the desire to see him, Josie made up her mind not to call him back and turned her mobile off.

"You seem on edge today," Libby said, "as they prepared to leave the office for their drink. Not worried about the job interview are you."

"Nope it's not that, haven't had a chance to even think about it. It's…well, Max phoned and wanted to see me tonight…" her voice trailed off.

"You idiot, I wouldn't have minded if you wanted to see him, we could do this again."

"It wasn't that, Lib. It's just that he calls when it suits him and expects me to be available for sex - great though it is. I have more self-respect than that though it hasn't always felt like that over the past few months."

"Come on," said Libby. "Let's go to Harry's Bar, you need a few Margheuritas. That will put Max out of your mind and hopefully Matt out of mine."

Several Margheuritas later the girls parted company and Josie headed drunkenly home on the Métro. When she arrived at the flat, Chrissie abruptly leapt up from the dining table.

"Where have you been? Your mobile's been off all evening and Max has been ringing here trying to get hold of you."

"I hope you told him I was out with a gorgeous, hunky, rich Frenchman who has swept me off my feet and wants me to have his babies," replied Josie, slurring quite a bit.

"You're pissed," said Chrissie laughing. "So you know he's been trying to get hold of you then? Actually, he was quite rude when I answered the phone, implied I was lying when I said I didn't know where you were. I told him that I thought you had a late business meeting. Where have you been by the way?"

"Thanks, yes I did know he was trying to get hold of me which is why I left my phone off and I've been to Harry's bar with Libby. Didn't realise how late it was," she said glancing at the clock. It was already 9.30 pm and they had left work at 5.00 pm.

"I've decided not to be at Max's beck and call any more. I will call him tomorrow and explain that I was tied up all day and suggest we meet later in the week. If he can't make it then tough, there are new rules in this relationship, if you can call it that. And on that note, I am going to bed before I fall over."

Chrissie laughed as she watched Josie stumble to her bedroom. When she checked on her later, Josie was sprawled across her bed, half undressed. Chrissie wrapped the quilt around her, poured a large glass of water which she thought Josie would need in the morning and switched off the light.

"She'll regret it," thought Chrissie to herself as she left the room. "Both the drink and not getting back to Max I know she will."

The next morning, Josie was suffering with a horrendous hangover and instantly regretted the Margheuritas but not, surprisingly for Chrissie, getting back to Max.

"Look, I meant what I said last night," she told her friend, "I wasn't that drunk. I don't want him to think I'm a pushover, of course I am but I don't want him to know it. I'll call him when I get to work and suggest we meet later in the week. If he can't make it, it's his loss. Now I need coffee, a shower and a huge pain au chocolat."

Once she had a quiet moment in the office, Josie nervously dialled Max's mobile. She never phoned him on his work or home number, just in case a colleague or Anna picked up the messages - she had strict instructions.

She hoped the mobile would go onto answer machine but Max answered after the second ring. "Max," said Josie putting on her brightest, bubbliest voice. "Sorry I didn't get back to you yesterday but I was out with clients all day and then dinner. Didn't get home until the early hours. Chrissie left a note to say you called but it was so late, I didn't want to disturb you."

Josie hadn't told Max exactly what she did in her job and always managed to hype it up a bit.

"OK," he replied coldly. "I thought you were avoiding me. You haven't called."

"You don't like me to call you," she replied without thinking.

"Well you can call on my mobile during the day time."

Sure but I can't call you evenings and weekends thought Josie to herself, because of horrible Anna.

"Fine, if you want me to call you I will but I don't like to disturb you at work and my days are hectic too, especially with the move to London."

"Move to London," spluttered Max, "Are you moving to London?"

Josie hesitated. She could be truthful or lead him on a bit here. "Well, I'm not sure yet. JC only told us last week that it was definite. So I'm looking at a number of options at the moment to see what's best for me. Actually, I have a job interview later this week at…"

"Well you don't let the grass grow under your feet do you," said Max sharply. "When were you going to tell me?"

"When I saw you?" replied Josie.

"Well you could have seen me yesterday," said Max petulantly. "You know Monday is our evening."

The conversation was making Josie angry.

"Well I'm sorry Max but believe it or not, I do not sit around waiting for you to call me to arrange to meet for a night of fucking. I do have a life you know."

"OK, I'm sorry. It was just the shock of hearing that you may go back to London. I didn't realise…"

A few months ago, Josie would have been dancing around the room to hear Max say these words but today she was still feeling used by him.

"You know we have such great times together Josie," he continued, "I just can't bear the thought of giving you up."

"I'm your love drug," she thought and you need a fix. Then almost giggled out load when Max seemed to read her thoughts.

"How are you fixed later this week," asked Max. "How about Thursday, I'll cook you a meal and you can tell me all about your plans."

"Thursday," said Josie, "how can you meet me on a Thursday. What about Anna?"

Again, the words were out before she thought about it.

"Anna's away on a course from tomorrow but I'm away on business until Thursday. That's why I wanted to get hold of you, we could have had last night and Thursday night… I'm also off Friday so I wondered if you could take the day off?"

Josie was in turmoil. This was what she had dreamed of. Real time with Max not just sex… "Be cool," she said to herself. "Don't let him play all the tunes."

"I'm sure Thursday evening will be fine, my interview isn't until 5.00 pm so I'll have to go home, change and then meet you. But I'm not sure about Friday, we're so busy at work and I had a lot of time off before Christmas. I'll have to check and get back to you."

"OK gorgeous," replied Max his spirits restored, "text me about Friday as soon as you can and if you can't make it I'll probably come into work. See you Thursday, can't wait. Bye."

"Bye," said Josie and hung up, completely confused.

"I caught the gist of that," said Libby who's desk was opposite Josie's, "what's happening then?"

Josie explained what Max had said. "I don't know what to do, Libby" she said. "It's what I've dreamed of but I really want to stand my ground and make him realise that he can't just click his fingers and I'll come running. I'd love to spend the day with him on Friday and maybe this will be the only chance we ever have… who knows. Oh God, what shall I do?"

"As I told you last night, life's too short to miss out on opportunities. Go for it Josie if you don't, you'll always regret it. What do you have to lose… a day in your life and you never know it could be an eye opener for him. I know, I'll phone you loads of times on your mobile, pretending to be customers and other men, just to get him going. It will be a laugh and it won't do you any harm."

"OK, Libby, sounds good to me. I just need to get the OK from JC. I think I'll tell him I have the job interview on Friday instead. What do you think?"

Libby agreed and so Josie booked Friday off but left it until the end of the day to confirm with Max by text that she could spend Friday with him. He sent a text straight back saying that was great and that he'd see her around 8.00 pm on Thursday at his place.

When Josie arrived home that evening she told Chrissie what had happened. "Oh not Thursday," said Chrissie. "Don't you remember? I told you last night. Claude phoned and the guys have invited us out for dinner and then a tour of the air traffic control centre. I did tell you Josie."

"Oh shit," she replied, "that sounds like fun."

"What are you going to do?"

"Well I can't cancel now, I've confirmed everything with Max. You'll have to go without me but don't tell them where I am. I quite liked Christian and I don't want him to think I'm in a relationship, because I'm not."

"You are on your own Josie," replied Chrissie, shaking her head sadly, and Josie sensed her friend was annoyed.

"You'd better invite Libby?" said Josie.

"I'll ask her but I didn't think she was too struck on our air traffic control friends the other night."

"Well I think she'd appreciate the offer, I think she finds it a bit lonely living on her own, especially when she sees how the two of us get on." Josie was trying her best to appease Chrissie. She knew her flatmate didn't approve of Max but Josie just couldn't help herself. She was infatuated.

Josie knew that Chrissie didn't approve of Libby's relationship with Matt either. Chrissie came from a very stable and close knit family unit and sometimes Josie felt that her flatmate could be a bit naive when it came to the complexities of relationships. Everything was black and white in Chrissie's world and all her relationships to date had been stable and school boyish.

"You're probably right," said Chrissie. "I know I didn't enjoy living on my own. Probably why she spends so much time around here!"

"Was that a dig," thought Josie to herself. She did sometimes sense some friction between Chrissie and Libby but never really understood why.

Later that evening Chrissie called Libby who was delighted to be invited along on Thursday. Josie couldn't hear everything they were saying as the land line was in the hallway but from what she picked up, she thought they were talking about her and Max.

"Libby's coming and will probably stay over on Thursday as you won't be here Josie. It will be easier for the guys to drop us off and for her to get to work the next day."

Josie felt a pang of jealousy. The girls were going to have a fabulous evening with a bunch of interesting, good looking guys…. How often did that happen? And what was she doing? Succumbing to the sexual cravings of the love of her life.

"I'm being too dramatic thought Josie… I am not succumbing to anything. I am going to spend a night and a whole day with a guy I fancy like hell, whom I am probably in love with…. (scary!). What can be better?"

When Thursday came, the interview was the last thing on Josie's mind. She just wanted to get the day over with and see Max. It didn't help that Chrissie and Libby kept on about their evening out with Christian, Claude and Yves. "There'll be other times," thought Josie, "especially if the girls have a good time."

Josie wore her new green dress and black jacket to work that day ready for the interview later. She also managed to book in a quick cut and blow dry at lunchtime, for Max rather than the job interview. The day dragged on and on but eventually 4.30 came and Josie left the office under the pretence of popping into the design studio. The company who had invited her for an interview were called 'Manganese' something or other and were based just next to the Parc Monceau, not too far from her flat.

The offices were impressive and Josie was shown into a large reception area and asked to wait a few moments. A short time later, a plump woman in her early forties came out of a set of double doors opposite the reception area. She had what was obviously a portfolio in her hands and gave Josie a condescending look as she walked past her.

A well dressed woman approached Josie and said her name, "Josephine James?"

"Oui, ça c'est moi - that's me," Josie stood up and shook her hand.

"I am Madame Fontaine, I will be interviewing you along with our Marketing Director, Monsieur LaFleuve. Did you bring your portfolio."

Josie was mortified. She hadn't even realised that she needed one. The job was for a marketing executive and she had exaggerated her marketing experience on the application form.

"I am really sorry," she replied quickly. "As I mentioned in the application form, I am looking for alternative employment as my current company is moving back to London in March. I have been in London myself since Tuesday organising the move and have just flown back. I was hoping to pass by the office to pick up my portfolio but unfortunately the flight was delayed and I really didn't want to be late for the interview. I can, of course, drop it off for you tomorrow if you would like me to."

Madame Fontaine gave her a sceptical look and raised a quizzical eyebrow archly. Not a great start Josie thought to herself.

From that moment on the interview went from bad to worse. A few minutes into the questions, Josie realised that she knew virtually nothing about marketing, although several times Monsieur LaFleuve commented on her excellent French.

The interview lasted 30 minutes and it was one of the longest in Josie's life. At the end, Monsieur LaFleuve asked her if she had any questions for them. She was tongue tied. Suddenly something popped into her mind from an article she had read a while ago about interview techniques. "I've just the one question really. In addition to the role you outlined in the job description and the expectations you have explained today, what, in your opinion, would make me want to take this job over another one?"

Madame Fontaine looked totally affronted but Monsieur LaFleuve laughed out loud.

"Well Mademoiselle James, you may not know much about marketing but I admire your belief in yourself."

Josie beamed. She knew she had performed abysmally in the interview but felt she had at least redeemed herself in the eyes of the Marketing Director.

He replied by reeling off the benefits of working for the company and Josie thanked him for clarifying that.

A stony faced Madame Fontaine showed Josie back to the reception area where a nervous young man was sitting on the same sofa where she had found herself earlier. She gave him what she thought was an encouraging smile but it only served to make him look more nervous.

"Merci beaucoup, Madame," said Josie, "Et Au revoir". She didn't mention the non-existent portfolio she had promised to drop off the next day. She knew she had blown the interview and anyway tomorrow she was spending the day with Max and she couldn't wait.

It was 6.30 pm by the time she arrived home. She ran herself a hot bath and relaxed for just a few minutes before hopping out to put on fresh make up, her outfit for the evening and to pick up the overnight bag she had prepared the night before. She wanted to call at the 24-hour deli on her way to the Métro to pick up some olives and red wine (Max's favourites). She thought champagne would be a bit over the top, as if celebrating something. But olives to have with their aperitifs and red wine for the main course seemed just right.

Chrissie had phoned Claude earlier in the day and arranged to meet at one of the girls' favourite Bistro's on the Rue Mouffetard. Fortunately, Claude knew the restaurant well.

The Rue Mouffetard is on the outskirts of the Latin quarter and is simply full of restaurants of different nationalities and tastes. Waiters stood outside, tempting people in with offers of one or two free aperitifs or free desserts. The girls enjoyed strolling down the street, checking out the ménus conseillés (set menus) before deciding which type of food they fancied. There was however one French restaurant which was a particular favourite. The girls had been there so many times the owner, Jean Claude, knew them well and always ensured they had free wine or extra-large portions. The restaurant was called La Grénouille (as it specialised in frogs legs). It was the first place Josie had tried frog's legs and though they tasted OK there was just nothing to them, no substance.

Chrissie had booked the restaurant in agreement with Claude and they were due to meet there at 8.00 pm (just when Josie would be arriving at Max's).

"What are you going to tell the guys," she asked Libby who had just arrived to drop off her overnight bag and travel to the restaurant with Chrissie.

"What do you want us to say," asked her friend.

"Tell them I am out with clients and couldn't' get out of it. You can bullshit Libby."

"OK but it seems a bit unfair to lie to them. They seem like nice guys. Also, if Christian thinks you're seeing someone else, it may make him even more interested!"

"I just don't want you to go into the why's and wherefores'," replied Josie.

"Anyway, must dash, I'm off via the deli. Have a fabulous evening and don't forget Libby, lots of texts and calls tomorrow. I have to keep Max on his toes you know."

"Well you have a lovely time," replied Libby, "and give me a call tonight if you get a chance."

"I will call, but hopefully not until tomorrow afternoon, which is when I'm planning to get out of bed. I hope Max has the same plan in mind."

She left the girls with a knowing wink and headed for the deli and then the Métro. She was around 10 minutes early at Max's apartment and really didn't want to seem too keen so she stopped in a café on the corner of his street and ordered a gin and tonic.

Josie could see Max's apartment from the café. She sipped her drink, warmly anticipating the evening ahead. She couldn't help but smile at the thought of a whole evening and day with Max. She glanced up the street towards his apartment block and was shocked to see Max emerge onto the street with his arm around Jane, Anna's best friend.

He gave her the traditional three kisses on the cheek and then Jane left in the direction of the Métro. Josie was flabbergasted - Max and Jane? He always spoke very highly of her and Josie had always had suspicions that he fancied her but what was that all about?

Josie didn't know what to do. It could be totally innocent. Jane was Anna's best friend and could have just called around on the off chance but they seemed very close. What should she do? Confront Max and tell him that she saw them or pretend it hadn't happened. Josie ordered another gin and tonic to steady herself. She wished she could call Chrissie or Libby to see what they thought but it wouldn't be fair and anyway she sensed that Chrissie in particular thought she was being stupid over Max.

Whilst sipping her second gin and tonic, which really hit the spot, she had skipped lunch to go to the hairdressers. Josie decided what to do. If Max acknowledged that Jane had been there, then it was fine and supposedly innocent. If he didn't, then Josie was going to say that she saw Jane in the Métro and they had a brief chat. "That would scare the pants off him," she thought to herself, finishing off her drink and feeling better for having a plan of action.

Five minutes later after a quick check of her hair and makeup in the loo, she rang the buzzer of Max's apartment. He answered straight away. "Hi gorgeous is that you?"

"It may be," replied Josie, "it depends who you were expecting."

Max laughed and pressed the buzzer to let her in. He was waiting for her at the door and immediately took her in his arms and gave her a passionate kiss and hug. "Wow, you look fabulous,

Josie. I've been thinking about you all day. I simply couldn't wait for this evening."

"Really," she replied, noting the lack of preparation for the romantic dinner he was supposed to have prepared for her. She was just about to tell him that she had bumped into Jane when he beat her to it.

"I'm running a bit late I'm afraid Josie. Anna's friend Jane called around, she had forgot Anna was away. She's in a right mess, having problems with her boyfriend and so poured her heart out to me. Sounds like a right bastard, playing away and all that."

The words were out before Max realised what he had said. Josie just looked at him.

"Well, I guess I'm the pot …..Anyway there's far more to it than that, heaps of personal stuff poor love. So take a pew, put the television on and I'll make you a nice gin and tonic.

Josie didn't really want another gin but didn't feel she could turn it down. She also realised she hadn't managed to get a word in edgeways. Was Max acting in a strange, nervous way?

She followed him into the kitchen and handed him the bag of olives and wine. "Wasn't sure what was on the menu," she said, "so I brought these."

"Thanks babe, pop the wine in the rack over there, I've already opened one to let it breathe and there's a bowl for the olives in the cupboard just in front of you."

Josie was now in her element. The dilemma of Jane no longer seemed to matter and this felt like real domesticity. "Can I do anything else?" she asked once she'd found a bowl for the olives and slotted the wine into a space in the already full wine rack which was an integral part of Max's modern kitchen.

"Nope all under control. Steak, salad and fresh baguette, followed by a surprise for dessert. You can make a salad dressing though if you like. I know you have a secret recipe!"

Josie had picked up tips working in bars and hotels as a student which she reeled out from time to time.

Whilst Max put the steaks under the grill and prepared a mixed salad, Josie found the ingredients she needed to make her special French dressing: garlic glove cut in half and rubbed around the dish, baby onion chopped finely and sprinkled around the bowl, three tablespoons of oil, one tablespoon of white wine vinegar, a teaspoon of mustard and salt and pepper. She tasted the dressing with her little finger and then dipped it again in the dressing and placed it on Max's lips.

"Mm Delicious," he said, "just like you."

His hands moved onto her face, gently caressing her neck, her shoulders, and then her buttocks. "Mmm, stockings, just as I like you," he said, caressing her buttocks and legs seductively. He kissed her full on the mouth, his tongue teasing her lips and the tip of her tongue.

"Plenty of time for that," he said pulling away from her. "Let's eat."

Josie was disappointed she had been getting really turned on watching Max cooking and working alongside him. But she knew he was right and the anticipation was every bit as exciting as the act itself. They sat at the dining table, next to the double balcony door. Max's apartment was on the 8th floor with stunning views over Paris. It was too cold to open the doors but this didn't stop Josie enjoying the spectacular view.

"You are so lucky living here," said Josie. "The apartment, everything is fabulous. It just makes ours seem so dowdy by comparison."

"Well it helps that the company pays," replied Max. "I'm on secondment from the UK, the company owns the flat and so I don't have to pay any rent. I pay the local taxes and bills but they foot the main bill, otherwise I couldn't afford it."

Josie hadn't realised that Max was on secondment. "So you could be moved back to the UK at any time," she asked him, hoping this wasn't the case.

"Not exactly," he replied, "I was here originally on a three year contract but it's recently been extended for another two years. I must be doing something right, steak OK?"

"Delicious thanks," she replied, reflecting that there was so much she didn't know about this man and his life. She knew very little about his family or past. Theirs had always been such a physical relationship that there hadn't been much time for talking.

"How did the interview go by the way," he asked, pouring Josie another large glass of wine.

Josie related the whole event and Max was laughing at the end. "How on earth did you think you'd get away with it," he asked. "I mean, what exactly do you do in your current job."

Josie didn't want to go into too much detail. Basically she was a 'humble' secretary but working for JC involved a lot more than that. She avoided the direct question by explaining that there were varying approaches to marketing and that the firm she had the interview with were operating way in the distant past. She guessed Max wasn't necessarily that interested and so changed the subject to more general matters.

Once the main course was over Max insisted on clearing the table himself and then brought in pudding. Crème caramel, Josie's favourite.

"I didn't make it myself," he said, "but I remembered how much you like it."

Josie was bowled over. He had remembered her favourite pudding and had made this special effort for her. Although a small gesture in the grand scheme of things, to Josie this was extra special.

"Are you OK," Max asked, as Josie had just stared at him and then the dessert and then back at him.

"Fine, I just can't believe you knew this was my favourite. I don't even remember telling you."

"Ah, so you don't remember telling me that your fantasy was for me to cover you in your favourite pudding, crème caramel, and then lick it all off?"

Josie blushed, a rare occurrence for her. She did vaguely recollect this conversation but when she met Max they usually drank so much that she couldn't always remember what she had said.

Josie emboldened by the gin and red wine stood up and began to unbutton the gold, silk shirt she had worn for the occasion. "I do remember and now is the time to realise that particular fantasy."

She stood close to Max and slowly removed her shirt and then unzipped her skirt and let it fall to the floor. She stood in front of him, dressed only in a black lace bra and knickers, suspenders, stocking and high heels.

Max grabbed her by the waist and pulled her to him, sinking his mouth in the mound between her breasts. With one hand he pulled aside her panties and began to massage her already swollen clitoris, with the other, he removed her breasts from the bra cups, leaving them balanced on the black, lace fabric and began licking each nipple with the tip of his tongue.

After a few seconds of this exquisite pleasure, Josie pulled

Max's head back from her breasts and kissed him hard and full on the lips. He stood up, picked her up in his arms and carried her over to the rug in front of the fireplace where they had made love many times before. Returning to the table he picked up the dish of crème caramel. He quickly undressed, down to his boxers and Josie could see his huge erection, the tip of his penis practically sticking out from the belt of his pants. She desperately wanted to feel him inside her but was completely turned on by the thought of her crème caramel fantasy becoming a reality.

He knelt down beside her and began caressing her breasts again with his tongue before slowly removing her bra. He then slid her panties off, leaving the stockings and suspenders in place (his preference). He kissed her again hard and fast and then began to rub the crème caramel into her body. He started with her shoulders and then her breasts, her stomach, belly button, thighs and then all over her labia and clitoris.

"I hope you've saved some for me," said Josie, thoroughly turned on as Max ate her favourite dessert from the most intimate parts of her body. "Don't worry, there's plenty left," he said, "massaging the soft, yellow liquid into her breasts and belly. He then started an onslaught with his tongue, pausing now and again to kiss her so she could taste the sweetness on his mouth. Josie had never experienced anything like it. "Why was it always so good with him?" she said to herself, I'll bet he couldn't do this with Anna!"

Josie allowed herself to be swept up with the sensations of Max licking the crème caramel off her body and sharing it with her at the same time. The delays between kisses and licking the dessert off her body meant that her orgasm took longer to come but once it did, Josie's whole being was alight with a tingling sensation she had never experienced before. As quickly as the orgasm subsided, she felt herself coming again as Max continued to lick the sweet liquid from her very wet vagina.

"The taste of you combined with the crème caramel is absolutely amazing," he whispered as his mouth moved back up her belly to her breasts, neck and mouth. Kissing him back with equal urgency, Josie rolled Max over onto his back and began her own onslaught.

She continued to kiss him hard and fast for a few minutes, before removing her tongue from deep within his mouth to lick the sides of his lips, his ears, neck, nipples, belly button and then, as he was still wearing his boxers, she simply ran her tongue the length of his encased shaft, breathing hard, making him pant in anticipation.

"God that is such a turn on," murmured Max, getting even harder as Josie continued her heavy breathing and sucking over his boxers. A few minutes later, she quickly removed his pants, practically ripping them off him. After a few gentle licks to the head and the shaft of his penis, Josie reached over and took a handful of the crème caramel in her hand. She totally ignored the rest of his body. Concentrating on his penis and testicles she gently massaged the soft, yellow liquid into his private parts, covering every millimetre. She then used her tongue to spread the dessert along the length of his shaft and into the slit at the tip of his cock. His groans of pleasure told Josie she was hitting the spot.

As Max had done before her, once she had sucked and licked for a few minutes she kissed him full on the mouth. Deep lingering kisses so he could taste the sweetness of her own mouth. After a few minutes of this exquisite sharing, Max cleverly moved his mouth so it was close to Josie's vagina. Without words, she moved towards Max's mouth and they then licked and sucked each other until Josie came again.

She knew she needed to feel Max's deep inside her. It was like an ache. Moving away from his mouth, she pushed him back onto the rug and mounted him, her legs elongated either side of his. To pull himself deeper inside her, Max wound his own legs around her waist. It felt as though they were one. Josie could tell from Max's continued thrusting that he was nearly there himself.

"Stop a second," she said. Without releasing him from inside her, Josie turned around and put her knees either side of Max's legs. He grabbed her waist with one arm and began to massage her nipples with the other. Josie cried out that she was coming again and she could tell from the tension in Max's legs and the hardness of him inside her that he was coming too.

Once they had both recovered from the intensity of their orgasms, Max held Josie gently in his arms.

"That was sensational," he told her, continuing to kiss and caress her gently. "Where did you learn tricks like that?"

"Tricks," Josie was mortified. "It's not about tricks," she replied angrily, "it's just with you, it feels natural. Nothing is planned"

"Sorry babe," I didn't mean to offend you it's just with Anna it's nothing like this.

"So why do you stay with her?" asked Josie quietly, still upset that Max thought that she practised what to her just seemed to be instinctive.

"Habit, I suppose," he replied tentatively. "We've been through quite a lot together really. There are things I haven't told you about, like when I was nearly sacked and Anna stuck by me. I owe her a lot."

"But that's no basis for a relationship. Just because you feel you owe someone."

"I know, but Anna knows me. Warts and all. You only see one side of me Josie. With you I'm terrified of falling off that pedestal you've put me on."

Josie was about to protest but realised he was right. She did put him on a pedestal and really she only knew him physically. They talked, of course they did but in reality she knew very little about him.

"Anna and I were at University together in Manchester," he continued. "But we only started going out together when we met up again over here. We sort of just fell into a routine really as neither of us knew many people then. As we made more friends, they always considered us to be a couple. So we just drifted into it."

"Does she make you happy?" Josie asked moving away from his embrace to look him square in the face.

"Now that's a leading question," he replied avoiding the question.

Josie asked him again.

"Sometimes, most times. We just know each other so well. She's not sexy like you Josie but we are comfortable together."

"Well, I can't compete with comfortable," said Josie standing up and reaching for her clothes. "To be honest Max, if you had said you were in love with her and this was just a fling or something like that I would get it. But to settle for comfortable is just wrong. What about passion and excitement."

Josie realised that, in fact, Max was in a win, win situation. He had stability with Anna and passion with her - the best of both worlds.

"You're right Max I don't know you at all. But what I've learnt this evening is that I don't know if I even want to. You want the best of both worlds. Unfortunately, that doesn't make me feel great."

"Come on Josie, don't be like that. I've never lied to you or pretended that I could offer you more than this."

Josie looked at him sitting on the rug in front of the fire - the rug on which they had made love many times. His face flushed and with bits of crème caramel sticking to his now limp penis, he looked ridiculous.

"True, you haven't," said Josie," but I deserve more than this. I just didn't realise it before."

With that, she picked up her clothes and headed for the bathroom. She rested her flushed face against the mirror and a tear trickled down her cheek. "A tear for myself and for what might have been," she said to herself.

Josie splashed water over her face, wiping the remains of the sticky dessert off her body before getting dressed. Once she was ready, she sat for a few minutes on the edge of the bath, planning the best exit. Would Max try to stop her? Did she want to go? They had such great plans for the next day, all ruined.

As Josie opened the bathroom door the phone in Max's living room rang. He answered it and Josie took the opportunity to slip into the hallway to retrieve her coat and bag and leave. She couldn't help but overhear his conversation.

"Hello babe, you OK?"

"Anna," said Josie to herself quietly slipping on her boots.

"Well Jane, as it turns out, looks like I can get out of my appointment tomorrow. Great, see you then. You're sure Anna doesn't suspect a thing?"

Josie couldn't believe it. He had just finished having sex with her and because things didn't go his way, he was taking up with his girlfriend's best mate. "Bastard absolute bastard," muttered Josie as she opened the front door and took great pleasure in slamming it thunderously behind her.

She didn't glance up at Max's balcony as she headed quickly for the underground station. Fortunately a train came straight away and within 15 minutes she was home.

"Shit, shit, shit," she said to herself as she let herself into the quiet, dark apartment. It was only 10.30 pm and the others wouldn't be back for ages and Libby was expecting to sleep in her bed. "Tough," she said out loud heading for the kitchen for a bottle of wine.

When the girls returned a few hours later, they found Josie sprawled over the sofa, completely out of it, still wearing her coat.

"Looks like things didn't go according to plan," said Chrissie when she saw the state Josie was in.

Libby covered her with a quilt, put a glass of water on the coffee table and left her on the sofa.

The next morning she woke to the sound of the girls getting up to get ready for work. Once she realised where she was and recalled the events of the night before, she covered her head with the quilt and pretended to sleep. But Chrissie was having none of it.

"Come on you," she said as she shook Josie by the shoulder. "A strong cup of coffee is what you need."

Josie peeped out from under the quilt. "Just leave me to die in peace, please…" she said to her friend.

"No chance, we saw what state you were in last night. What happened then?"

Josie explained briefly about the conversation she had with Max about Anna and told Chrissie that she realised she deserved more than that in a relationship. She didn't mention the conversation she'd overhead with Jane.

"About bloody time too," replied Chrissie as Libby came into the living room. "Josie's seen sense…. and realised what we've been trying to tell her for ages… Max has been using you Josie, but you had to see it for yourself."

Libby gave Josie sympathetic looks. Chrissie had been less understanding but in her heart she knew Chrissie was right.

"Enough already," she said trying to make light of the situation. "Tell me about your evening, how was it?"

The girls had had a great evening with the air traffic controllers. After their meal, which the men had paid for, they drove them to Orly and visited the air traffic control tower. The atmosphere in the tower was very intense and made the girls realise the importance of the job they did. Essentially they literally held people's lives in their hands. The visit was brief as they couldn't disturb the controllers on duty and afterwards they all went to Claude's flat for coffee and cake.

"And Chrissie and Claude spent an awfully long time checking out the etchings in his bedroom," said Libby laughing.

Chrissie threw a cushion at her. "He's really lovely and we did have a snog but that was it, for now. He's asked me out tomorrow night in fact - just me and him, not you lot…."

"Are you going," Libby asked.

"Maybe, haven't said yes or no yet. I probably will but I can't let him know I'm too keen."

Josie groaned, she should take a tip from Chrissie's play book. Play it cool and not be full on all the time. But she couldn't help it. She put 100% into everything, it was in her nature.

"Well, while you lot go off to work, I am heading for the shower and then back to bed. "Tell you what though. As I now have a free day, I will go shopping and cook you both a delicious, nutritious meal this evening. How about that?"

"Sounds great," said Libby. "I'll need to go home first though and I won't stay overnight as I have loads to do in the flat… like cleaning and washing. Fancy the cinema on Saturday evening?"

The cinemas in Paris were wonderfully modern and showed all the latest French, British, American and foreign films in 'original languages' always with sub titles. The girls usually went to the cinema at least once a week and saw a variety of films which they would never have seen if they had stayed in the UK.

They had, of course, seen most of the major US blockbusters as well as all the Harry Potter and Twilight movies. But more often than not they opted for an original French film or an off the wall Spanish or Italian movie based on film reviews in the local newspapers.

Josie agreed immediately but Chrissie declined. "I think I'll put Claude out of his misery and agree to this hot date."

Once the others had left for work, Josie finished her coffee, took off her clothes, had a quick shower, put on her favourite, warm pyjamas and got into her own bed, which Libby had carefully tidied up earlier. She surprisingly felt good about herself. Things had come to a head with Max and they had needed to. She still had strong feelings for him. "Lust rather than love," she thought to herself. "But I can't be second best to 'comfortable, that's just not right."

This was the start of the rest of her life. At the back of her mind she seemed to remember saying that to herself many times before. She would get a new job, a slimmer figure and a new man. She also recalled Chrissie saying how disappointed Christian had been when he realised Josie wasn't joining them last night. Perhaps he could prove to be a worthy distraction from Max she thought as she drifted off to sleep.

CHAPTER 6

Josie was woken at midday by the sound of the phone ringing. She had dozed on and off all morning, conscious of the traffic going by in the street and movement in the flat next door.

She jumped out of bed and picked up the phone in the hallway. It was JC.

"Salut Josie ç'est moi, JC. I've been trying to get you on your mobile but it's off, thought you may still be in the interview. How did it go?."

Josie had completely forgotten about the interview and that she had told JC it was today.

"Terrible," she replied, "but I did make the MD laugh."

"Good for you. Look I know you have a day off but I would really like to see you and Libby today together if possible."

"OK," said Josie. "Give me an hour and I'll be there."

"Great but don't expect any overtime!"

Josie had her second shower of the day and arrived at the offices as fresh and lively as she could be. Libby was surprised.

"What are you doing here, it's your day off?"

"JC told me he needed to see us both together, so here I am. What's it all about?"

"No idea," replied Libby.

Within a few minutes JC came into their office with business on his mind.

He told them that the PR agency, Renseignements, which the company was using for the Brussels seminar was looking for a bi-lingual secretary and account administrator. With a view to the position becoming a bi-lingual account executive in due course. The Chairman was a personal friend of JC's and so he had mentioned Josie and Libby to him as possible candidates. If they were in agreement, then they could both be interviewed the following week.

"Thanks JC," said Josie, genuinely grateful, "it sounds great and from the dealings I've already had with them, they seem to be a very professional set up."

"What's the package?" asked Libby, ever the realist. Josie would just be happy to have a job she enjoyed in Paris. Libby was far more mercenary. "Probably because of her upbringing," thought Josie, "always competing with her four sisters."

"I'm not sure, Libby, and I know your forte is accounts but you never know. This may interest you."

Josie felt that JC was backing Libby rather than her. This seemed a little unfair as Libby had said she would stay with JC to help with the office move. As if reading Josie's mind Libby questioned JC.

"But what if they offer me this job, what about the office move?"

"I'm sure we can come to some arrangement," he replied.

Libby nodded and Josie could tell she was seriously considering the offer.

"Anyway, Muriel has said she can always help with the move."

The girls understood straight away. JC would have his mistress helping him instead of Libby which would suit him down to the ground. He was probably contemplating employing her in London, which would suit him too. Neither of them knew whether his wife was aware of the affaire or not. The whole set up was quite bizarre.

"I'll phone Jacques Fredet, the Managing Director and let you know when they want to see you both. Enjoy the rest of your day off, Josie. See you Monday."

Once the girls were alone, they speculated about JC's actions. "He knows I'm a qualified accountant," said Libby, "to be honest I'm not really interested in a bi-lingual secretarial job, no disrespect Josie, but it's not what I went through University to be."

"I know what you mean," replied Josie, "I've only ever seen secretarial work as a means to an end. And to be honest, this sounds promising for me. Still we'll see next week. Right, I'm off shopping now. See you later…. Don't be late."

"I won't, don't worry, what are you cooking?"

"Not sure yet, depends what I fancy in the supermarket, see you later."

Josie left the office to walk home via the supermarket which was at Place de Villiers, not far from their flat.

As she began walking she couldn't help but reflect on the previous evening. Even though she had walked out of his apartment, she was surprised to have not heard a word from Max. Then she remembered something JC had said. He'd been trying persistently to get hold of her on her mobile, but it was switched off. Josie rummaged around in her handbag and retrieved her mobile. She quickly switched it on and once she had a signal, the phone started 'beeping' furiously.

Eighteen missed calls and six messages. She checked the calls first. Three of them were from Max, the rest were voicemail telling her she had messages. There was JC's earlier message and one from Chrissie saying she'd be a bit late as her boss had asked her to stay on for a little while.

Max's messages started off with apologies for upsetting her and asking her to call him back, the second was less apologetic and the third downright angry.

"Tough," thought Josie, "he's the one who has been behaving badly." Though in the back of her mind she knew she hadn't exactly been an angel herself.

As she headed past the Gare St Lazare she stopped in her tracks as she glimpsed a familiar profile in one of the cafés opposite the station. It was Max with Jane and they were sitting side by side, very closely, with his arm draped casually over the back of her seat. Josie was tempted to storm into the café and confront them but her pride and common sense had the better of her and she carried on past quickly, turning her face away from the window in case they spotted her. She had been weakening when she heard Max's calls and had been contemplating texting him to say she needed time to think and would get in touch shortly but seeing him with Jane made her realise what a bastard he really was.

For the rest of the day, she busied herself shopping and preparing supper, lasagne with garlic bread, green salad and cheese for afters. But she couldn't resist dwelling on thoughts of Max and Jane. Josie kept picturing them having sex together. She actually found herself feeling sorry for Anna. Max obviously didn't understand the first thing about fidelity and any woman was going to have her work cut out trying to keep hold of him.

Libby arrived at the flat by 7 but by 7.30 there was still no sign of Chrissie.

"We'll start without her and I can warm hers up later if necessary," said Josie who had already had three glasses of wine. "I don't want to get drunk again tonight and this is slipping down far too easily."

She poured Libby another glass and then began serving supper. Just as they sat down, Chrissie came in.

"Sorry," she said taking off her coat, "God I'm starving. This smells lovely Josie, thanks."

"Have you been working until now?" asked Josie.

"Well, not working exactly," she replied and began to explain why she was late. "My boss, Monsieur Dupré, asked me to stay after work for a chat. It was quite bizarre. He has a son, Thierry, who lives with his ex-wife somewhere near Rennes. Anyway, Thierry is coming to Paris for a while and Monsieur Dupré, has asked me to show him around a bit. I couldn't exactly refuse. Anyway he may be dishy and he's obviously rich, being his daddy's son. The problem is that he wanted me to take Thierry out tomorrow night but I had already told Claude I would see him. So I told Monsieur Dupré that I had plans but that I could meet his son on Sunday night if he wanted. He's going to call me, Thierry that is, not Monsieur Dupré."

With that the phone rang. Chrissie jumped. "It can't be him already, can it?"

She left the table to answer the phone. "Daniel, how are you? We haven't heard from you in ages."

"Not since New Year's eve," thought Josie who could tell that the others were thinking the same thing. "Tomorrow evening? Sorry Daniel, we've made plans. I have a date and the others are off to the cinema. No it's no-one you know."

Chrissie knew Daniel had a soft spot for her but couldn't resist winding him up by being secretive about her many dates.

"Sure," she continued. "I'll pass her to you now. He wants to speak to you Josie."

Josie took the phone off Chrissie. "Hi Daniel, how are you? Good. Yes I know the feeling, mega busy at our place too, the office is moving back to London so I'm busy hunting for a new job. Your place? Sure, please ask. I've had one interview and have another lined up. Tomorrow evening. Of course, you're more than welcome to join us. We're not sure what we're going to see yet. I'm meeting Libby at the top of the escalator at the Arc de Triomphe at 6.30 pm so see you then. Bye."

"He sounded very sheepish," said Chrissie once Josie had hung up. "I hadn't realised until now how long it's been since we've seen him. He must still be embarrassed about New Year's Eve."

"My thoughts exactly," replied Josie. "Well I won't say anything unless he does. It's water under the bridge as far as I'm concerned."

Josie hadn't heard from Angie either since New Year but was grateful as she really didn't want to bother with her any more.

"Let's leave all this," said Chrissie. "I'll clear up in the morning as you cooked Josie, there's a good film starting at 9.00, let's watch that."

The film was a French classic starring Gérard Dépardieu and Fanny Ardent about a couple having an affair. Even though she had seen the film several times before, the storyline made Josie feel not only uncomfortable but also sad recognising once and for all that it was all over with Max.

"I'm going to love you and leave you," said Libby. "I want to make an early start tomorrow and I'll take the Métro now rather than a taxi later. See you tomorrow evening Josie. And you have a good time with Claude, Chrissie. Don't do anything I would do!"

"Mmm, we'll see. He is gorgeous, isn't he? You never can tell but Claude might very well get lucky tomorrow night!"

They both nodded, knowing what Chrissie was like. She liked the chase but once she had her victim snared, she usually lost interest pretty quickly. The girls watched the film but half way through Josie started to fall asleep. So she went to bed and Chrissie wasn't far behind her. They slept late the next morning and while Chrissie cleared away the supper things, Josie took their washing over to the launderette across the road.

"He never fails to give me the creeps, horrible man," Josie said upon returning to the flat.

"You always say that," said Chrissie. "I don't find him too bad."

"Well I think he prefers my thongs to your granny knickers," replied Josie teasing her friend.

The girls spent a quiet day, pottering around the flat and just chatting and watching television. At 6.00 pm Josie left to meet Libby and Daniel on the Champs Elysées.

"Have a great time," she told Chrissie. "See you later ... maybe."

"Maybe indeed," smiled Chrissie. Claude was picking her up from the flat at 7.30 pm so once Josie had gone she was planning a soak before getting ready.

"Use some of my new bath oil," Josie told her. "It has little glittery bits in that sparkle on your body, looks great in a dim light."

Chrissie chucked a cushion at her. "Get of here so I can to make myself beautiful."

"You'll need a bit longer than an hour and a half," replied Josie quickly shutting the front door behind her before Chrissie could throw another cushion.

Daniel and Libby were already waiting for her at the exit to the Métro. They decided to go and see a recently released French film and started to queue 15 minutes before the doors opened. Unlike the British, the French don't really understand about queuing. As they chatted comfortably to pass the time, three French women came and stood alongside them in the queue. Once the doors opened, the women pushed in front of them.

"Hey," said Josie, "You can't do that."

The women ignored her. "Hey," said Josie again, "what about all the other people who are waiting. That's just damn rude."

One of the women turned to Josie and said, "Qui sont vous pour nous dire quoi faire." - "Who are you to tell us what to do?"

Fortunately, the people behind, also began to complain and eventually the three women moved to the back of the queue. The woman who had spoken earlier, threw Josie a filthy look and said, "I'll be waiting for you on the way out, bitch."

"I'm so very scared," replied Josie sarcastically.

Once in the cinema, Libby started to fret. "You shouldn't have said anything, Josie, they'll be waiting for us on the way out now."

"No they won't," she replied, "that sort are just bullies. But anyway I'm going to have a word with someone who works here, won't be a second."

Josie approached a young man wearing a smart cinema uniform. "Sorry to disturb you," she said to him, "but there was a bit of trouble with people trying to push in the queue before and when we made a fuss, they threatened to be waiting for us outside. We really don't want any trouble, so is there a side exit we could take at the end of the film?"

"Sure," said the young man. "I will meet you here at the end of the film and I'll let you out of the fire exit, it leads onto the Avenue Georges Cinque. But in exchange, will you meet me for a drink later on?"

Josie was taken aback. He was a good looking guy but a good few years younger than her, probably just turned eighteen she reckoned.

"I'm here with some friends," she replied diplomatically, "and we have plans later. But I'll give you my mobile number and you can call me to arrange another time."

"OK," he replied. "See you here later then."

"Don't you want my number then," she asked him.

His face lit up, "sure."

He took out his mobile and quickly typed in Josie's name and number. "Comme la paramour de Napoléon - like Napoleon's lover…." he said when she told him her name.

Josie just smiled, in fact she had given him a false number as he was far too young and sweet for her, but she didn't want to upset him either. Once the film was over, they met the young man, as agreed and he discretely let them out of the fire exit.

"I'll call you, tomorrow," he said to Josie once she thanked him for his help. Josie just winked at him. They had a quick drink in one of the bars on the Avenue Georges Cinque and Daniel picked up the tab, as usual, which was just as well as it was really expensive at the best of times, let alone on a Saturday night.

"We can't even seem to go to the cinema without something happening," said Libby. "I don't know Josie, life hasn't exactly been quiet since you came on the scene."

Josie couldn't tell if Libby was serious or not. She decided to give her the benefit of the doubt.

"They'll probably be waiting for us the Métro station," said Josie jokingly.

"Do you really think so?" Libby asked them. That broke the

ice and they all laughed.

"Well they'd be very sad, if they did," said Daniel, "but anyway let's not take the risk, I'll drive you home."

"But it's miles out of your way," said Josie, knowing that the only reason Daniel wanted to drop them home was to see if Chrissie was back from her date. He had been short of useless when Josie had spoken out in the queue. "He really is a wimp," thought Josie to herself. Still, if he was stupid enough to want to drive them home, then more fool him. Looking around the bar, Josie spotted a poster advertising a rugby club disco later that month. "Isn't that your rugby club, Daniel?" she asked him.

"Yes it is actually and I wondered if you'd all like tickets to go. It's a really good evening usually, especially after a French - English match. Libby declined the invitation saying she had visitors from the UK that weekend and it wouldn't really be their 'cup of tea'. Josie gave her a quizzical look, this was the first she'd heard that Libby had visitors and normally they told each other everything.

"Tell you again," Libby whispered to Josie winking theatrically.

"We'll have to check with Chrissie," said Josie, "but it's OK for me."

"We can check with Chrissie when I drop you off," he said.

Josie said that Chrissie was likely to be out very late but didn't elaborate as it was up to her friend, not her, to deal with Daniel. They left the bar and walked down the Champs Elysées towards the car park. They were all quiet, taking in the sights and sounds of one of Paris's busiest streets on a Saturday evening. It was still only January and quite a grey, dreary evening so it wasn't as busy as usual but there were still quite a few colourful and interesting people in the bars and cafés or just wandering along the pavements. It never failed to amaze Josie how much she loved 'people watching' over here.

"Everyone just seems that much more interesting … with one or two exceptions," she thought to herself glancing at Daniel. He was dressed in his usual brown and beige, cords, shirt, jumper, sandy hair in an unfashionable side parting. He had said nothing about New Year's Eve and had acted as if nothing untoward had happened, though he had been more quiet than usual.

Josie was determined not to let him in when he dropped her home. They dropped Libby first and within 15 minutes they were outside the girls' apartment."

"Thanks, Daniel," said Josie quickly stepping out of the car. "Really good of you to bring me home. Give us a call soon, OK."

As she walked up the steps, she could see Daniel, standing by his car looking forlornly up at the flat. She found it hard to understand why he kept chasing after Chrissie only to get knocked back every time.

"But it didn't stop him sleeping with Angie," she thought to herself.

Josie made herself a coffee, even though it wouldn't help her sleep, and sat down in the sitting room, mulling over the evening and events of the past few days. The rugby club do sounded good fun. Daniel had mentioned it before and so had Max. Josie thought the evening would be a bit of a test. She couldn't avoid Max forever as they did mix in similar circles, particularly when Daniel organised things. She hoped Chrissie would agree to come too as she didn't fancy going on her own with Daniel.

Josie finished her coffee and headed for her bedroom. In the hall, she saw that the answer phone was flashing. She pressed the replay button and there were two messages. One was from Thierry Dupré, Chrissie's employer's son, asking Chrissie to call him back. "Oops," thought Josie, "I hope Chrissie gets back at a reasonable time tomorrow to return that call. Otherwise she could be looking for a new job." The second was also for Chrissie from the same guy. His tone made Josie feel a bit uncomfortable as it was quite demanding and unreasonable.

The next morning, she was woken up by the sound of a key in the door. She glanced at her alarm clock, it was 10 am. She could hear Chrissie tip toeing around the apartment and so hopped out of bed to chat to her friend.

"Dirty stop out," she said to Chrissie who was in the kitchen putting the kettle on to boil.

"Look who's talking," her friend replied grinning. "How was your evening?"

"OK thanks but more importantly, how was yours?"

Chrissie grinned. "Fabulous, he is really lovely, caring, tender guy and very, very sexy."

"Come on then, tell all."

"No way," she smiled mischievously, "but put it like this. I will definitely be seeing Claude Beauchesnes again. He asked to see me this evening but I have to see that stupid Thierry bloke."

"He phoned last night twice" Josie told her, "asking you to call him back. You'd better put him out of his misery. He sounded a bit weird to me Chrissie."

"Oh great," said Chrissie, "I've found the love of my life and I have to play babysitter to the boss's weird son."

"Did you tell Claude about Thierry?"

"Of course, have to keep them on their toes. He was very cool about it. Although he insisted I call him when I get back from meeting Thierry ."

"Sweet," said Josie, meaning it. She had liked Claude when she met him, he seemed really together and confident, just what Chrissie needed. She told Chrissie about their evening, the row in the cinema queue, giving the young chap the wrong phone number and then Daniel driving them home and pining outside. Chrissie was chuckling as Josie recounted the evening's events with humour.

After breakfast, Chrissie called Thierry and he insisted on picking her up from the apartment at 7.00 pm promptly.

"Good," said Josie, "I'll get the chance to check him out."

"He'll probably run away scared…if you check him out!" she said. "Well, I didn't get much sleep last night so I'm for a few hours kip, what are you up to?"

"I think I'll pop out for a walk and pick up something for lunch from the deli." The girls tended to buy food as they went along, rather than planning a weekly shop. They kept meaning to get more organised but never actually got round to it. There was always, bread and cheese in the apartment along with supplies from the UK of beans and marmite, so they didn't go hungry. They just didn't always eat as healthily as they should.

Josie walked to Parc Monceau but it was too cold and damp to sit on the benches, so she headed home via the deli. She picked up some paté, a baguette, fresh tomatoes and some olives for Chrissie.

She strolled slowly back to the apartment, enjoying the fresh air and a rare quietness which was not normally prevalent in Paris. As she passed the launderette, which was closed on a Sunday, she saw the owner folding clothes from a dryer, holding each item up to inspect it and lingering far too long over the underwear. " Kinky as hell that one", said Josie to herself.

CHAPTER 7

Back at home Chrissie was on the phone, obviously to Thierry. When she finished the call she had a look of panic on her face.

"Oh my god, what a control freak," she said. "I was out cold and the phone ringing woke me. It was him, Thierry again. Explaining that we would be going to the cinema and then out for a meal and that I should dress appropriately. What did he think, that I would turn up in split crotch panties and a peep hole bra."

"Tempting, I know," said Josie, "but I'm not sure that's the impression you want to give him just yet! I must admit, I found his tone of voice quite scary when he left those messages for you yesterday. Just be careful, Chrissie, I know he's the boss's son and all that but you don't have to compromise yourself you know."

Chrissie nodded her head and then began rifling through the carrier bag which Josie had placed on the dining room table. After a quick lunch, the girls settled down to watch TV but within a few minutes, the doorbell rang.

"Who's that now?" said Chrissie who had been starting to doze in the chair.

"Bet your bottom dollar it's Daniel," said Josie, "checking up on you."

She was right. It was Daniel inviting them to join him for an ice cream at the drugstore near the top of the Champs Elysées. Neither of them really felt like going out but Daniel looked so forlorn, with a puppy dog, beseeching look in his eyes.

"OK," said Chrissie, "but we'll have to be back by around 5.00 pm as I'm entertaining my boss's son tonight and I have to get ready."

Daniel looked really miffed. "Were you out with him last night as well?" he asked her.

"No, I wasn't thank goodness," replied Chrissie but didn't elaborate any further. Whom she dated was none of Daniel's business. She knew he fancied her but she definitely didn't fancy him and he had never actually asked her out as such. She liked him as a friend and like Josie, sometimes felt a bit guilty about the way they used him. But he asked for it really, always offering to take them places and pay for everything … and he earned an absolute fortune so he could afford it.

The girls climbed into Daniel's car and he headed off for the Champs Elyées. The traffic was pretty quiet en route but was busier around the Arc de Triomphe. Daniel found a parking space just off the main avenue and they headed for the drugstore which was a weird sort of café inside a type of 'mall' which also included shops, fruit machines and a communications centre with lots of personal computers with access to the internet.

The ice creams in the drugstore were amazing and they all ordered different types so that they could try each others. Daniel, of course, picked up the tab.

"Have you decided about the rugby club do," he asked the girls.

"Oops, forgot to ask you Chrissie," said Josie explaining about the do.

"Not sure yet," she replied, "I may be away that weekend. When do you need to know Daniel?"

Daniel went red in the face. He obviously wanted to ask Chrissie where she was going, as did Josie, but he didn't dare.

"Well, end of this week really as the tickets go pretty quickly."

"OK, I'll let you know by the end of the week then."

By the time they had finished their ice creams and retrieved the car it was already 4.45 pm. Daniel took the girls home but they didn't invite him in, despite the dejected look on his face. In the flat, Josie collapsed on the sofa.

Chrissie headed for the bathroom and Josie dozed in front of the TV for an hour or so. Chrissie was ready by 6.30 pm and so she and Josie had a Kir Royale, just to unwind. At 7.00 pm prompt, the buzzer sounded and, of course, it was Thierry. Chrissie told him to come up and Josie pretended to be busy doing household, girlie things when he came into the sitting room.

It was all Josie could do to stop herself laughing. He was dressed very formally for a date at the cinema in old-fashioned grey slacks, a cloth beret, light blue shirt and navy blazer. His hair was cut extremely short and he had a pimply weasle-like face with a big beaky nose. He was no taller than Chrissie, herself only 5ft 5 inches in heels. He had brought her a bunch of flowers and as he handed them to her, Josie made a vomiting sign behind his back. Chrissie, obviously embarrassed by this gesture quickly shepherded him out of the apartment before Josie said something too untoward.

"Ugh," thought Josie as the door closed behind the departing couple, "creepy or what?"

Josie had the feeling that Chrissie would regret having agreed to go out with him. He seemed so dated, so formal and really up himself. "Oh well," she thought, "Chrissie can look after herself."

Josie wanted to wait up for Chrissie but by 11.30 pm she was too tired. Claude had phoned too and seemed really disappointed that Chrissie wasn't home. He asked Josie to get her to call him, no matter what the time was. At around 2.00 am she heard the front door open and hushed voices in the hallway. She got up and was amazed to see Chrissie, looking very dishevelled, mascara smudged around her eyes and her shirt ripped at the left arm. Daniel was with her.

"Oh my God, Chrissie, what happened?" she asked, putting an arm gently around her shoulders.

Chrissie sat down on the sofa and, without being asked, Daniel went into the kitchen. Josie could hear him opening and closing the kitchen cupboards until he returned with a glass of brandy for Chrissie and tea for all of them. Once she had drunk the brandy quickly she began to tell Josie what had happened.

Thierry had taken her to the cinema as planned but as soon as the lights went down, Thierry had started to get far too familiar. He started by putting his arm around her shoulders, then caressing her neck and rubbing his leg against hers. At one point his hand started to creep down towards her breast but Chrissie managed to shift in her seat, brushing his hand away from her body. She had felt quite uncomfortable throughout the film and was glad when it was over.

Outside the cinema she tried to get out of going for dinner but he was very insistent. Chrissie was feeling increasingly uneasy with Thierry. Nevertheless she was conscious that this was the boss's son. She gave him the benefit of the doubt and they went to a pizzeria close to the cinema. Chrissie wasn't very hungry, and desperate to get home, she just played with her food pushing it around the plate. The conversation was very stilted and after just 45 minutes, Thierry asked for the bill.

As they headed back to his car, Chrissie said that she could get a taxi home rather than take him out of his way but he was insistent that he drive her home. Her instincts were warning her not to get into the car. But she was also worried about offending him because of his father.

Against her better judgement, Chrissie did get into the car and they headed in the direction of Gare St Lazare and home. But as they approached the station, he took a small side road instead of the main road up towards rue de Villiers, and the flat. "It's straight up there," she said to him, trying to hide the panic in her voice.

"Ah bon, d'accord," he said, slowing the car down as if looking for a space to turn around.

"Je m'excuse, je ne suis pas au courant de ce secteur."

He pulled the car over as if to reverse but cut the engine. He then lunged at Chrissie, kissing her hard on the mouth and fondling her breasts roughly.

"Stop it" she shouted, trying to push him away.

"Vas-y, grande pute," he snarled, "tu sais que tu as envie de moi."

"Look at you in those jeans and that tight shirt, I know the signals. You've wanted me all evening."

Chrissie was horrified. She tried to open the car door but it was locked. As Thierry lunged at her again, she slapped him hard across the face.

His face red and angry, Thierry pulled at the front of Chrissie's shirt, popping the buttons and exposing her bra which he then pulled to one side revealing her left breast. His fingers grabbed at her nipple, kneading and twisting the tender tip leaving deep finger marks that would later bruise.

As Chrissie cried out in pain, he released her nipple and tore at the zip of her jeans, pulling it downwards and slipping his hand inside her panties. She tried to fight back, scratching at his arm trying to pull him off her.

Angry at her retaliation, Thierry hit Chrissie hard across the face, the signet ring that he wore on his little finger scratching her under the cheekbone.

Chrissie was momentarily dazed and Thierry seized the opportunity to release his thick erect penis from his pants. Grabbing a handful of hair he forced her face toward his penis, her lips brushed against the swollen head.

With survival at the forefront of her mind, Chrissie drew all her strength and determination into her right fist and literally thumped Thierry with all her force in his groin.

"Chienne foutue," he cried writhing back in the car seat in agony.

"Open this car now or I will call the police," she screamed at him, her mobile already in her hand the emergency services number clear on the display screen.

"Fuck off then you prick-tease," he shouted at her, spittle smattering her face. He unlocked the car with his key fob. Chrissie opened the door as quickly as possible, pulling up her jeans, and trying to pull her torn shirt around her exposed flesh.

Thierry reached out from the driver's seat and tried to grab her shirt sleeve to pull her back into the car. It ripped completely off her arm and Chrissie screamed out. Her shout unnerved him and he let go and Chrissie ran as fast as she could towards the station. In the brightness of the main hall she was conscious that people were staring at her. She headed for the toilets and inside looked at herself in the mirror. She was trembling and looked awful. Her shirt was torn and her face was streaked with blood where his ring had cut her.

Her first instinct was to call Josie but she would have to get a taxi to come and get her. So she called Daniel. She knew he would come for her. Chrissie quickly explained what had happened and within 30 minutes, he was outside the station. He called Chrissie, who had been waiting nervously in one of the locked cubicles, mobile in her hand. She came out of the station and Daniel just wrapped her up in his arms.

They sat in Daniel's car and Chrissie explained what had happened with Thierry. After a long time just sitting in the car and Chrissie reliving the horrible experience with Thierry she said to Daniel, "Please, just take me home."

Josie was appalled and wanted to call the police straight away but Chrissie was adamant that she didn't want the police involved. "But he practically raped you," said her friend, "he can't be allowed to get away with it."

"Oh he won't," replied Chrissie. "I did some thinking while I was waiting for Daniel and I am going to see his father first thing in the morning and tell him exactly what happened."

Josie wasn't sure that this was the greatest plan of action. What if Monsieur Dupré backed his son, Chrissie could lose her job.

"Well, I'll come with you," said Josie. "At least then it won't be just your word against Thierry's."

Chrissie was grateful for her friend's offer. None of them could sleep after the incident and the three friends chatted until 6.30 am when Daniel headed off for work. Chrissie followed him out into the hallway.

"Thanks Daniel," she said, giving him a peck on the cheek. "You really are a very good friend and I am so grateful that you came to my rescue. Believe me, I just can't thank you enough."

Daniel gave her a hug and there was a sad look in his eyes. "I would look after you, you know Chrissie."

Chrissie just nodded. She knew what he meant but she just couldn't imagine being anything other than friends with Daniel. She just didn't fancy him.

By 7.30 am the girls were ready to leave the apartment and head for Chrissie's office. Monsieur Dupré was always in early and Chrissie wanted to see him before the rest of the staff arrived. Within 20 minutes they were standing outside his office door. Chrissie knocked loudly and he shouted to come in.

His face lit up when he saw Chrissie but then looked bewildered when he saw Josie - he knew she was Chrissie's flat mate. "Bonjour mes belles, to what do I owe this honour?"

Chrissie tried not to show how nervous she was as she explained to Monsieur Dupré what had happened with his son the night before. Josie watched the older man's expression closely. He turned completely pale and his left eye started to twitch. Monsieur Dupré's hand moved to his eye and Josie thought he might be wiping away a tear.

"My dear girl," he said to Chrissie, coming around from

behind his desk and putting an arm around her. Chrissie flinched involuntarily.

"Sorry, but I can't believe Thierry would behave like that. I mean nothing like this has ever happened before…."

"He doth protest too much," thought Josie, watching Monsieur Dupré intently.

"I will of course speak to him. I promise this will never happen again."

"Monsieur Dupré," said Josie, moving closer to her friend and taking her hand. "You are very lucky that Chrissie didn't go to the police which was her decision and against the advice of her friends. I think you need to do more than speak to Thierry, don't you."

"Who else knows," asked Monsieur Dupré, a tremor of panic in his voice.

"Only Josie and our friend Daniel who came to pick me up after your son pushed me out of his car after the assault," replied Chrissie. "Look Monsieur Dupré, I really don't want to go to the police but I think you need to address this issue seriously with your son. He simply cannot behave like this."

"I know, I know, I've told him before, he can't behave like this."

Josie jumped in quickly, "so this has happened before then?"

"No, no, it's not that it's just that, well, since the divorce he has been spoiled by his mother. She simply can't say 'no' to him and so he thinks that he is entitled to anything he wants. Chrissie, I am really sorry. Nothing like this has ever happened before, I promise you. Otherwise I wouldn't have asked you to show him around. It's just that you are so bright and lively that I thought it may rub off on him. He can be so morose and moody… and maybe I painted the wrong picture of you to him. I am as much at fault as he is….." he trailed off.

"No Monsieur Dupré, this is not your fault at all. Your son cannot treat people, women like that … it's just not on."

Monsieur Dupré looked at her a deep sadness in his eyes. "Chrissie, I am so, so sorry. I wanted Thierry to come to Paris to get away from his mother but I'm not doing a very good job of being a father to him either. I work long hours and rather than show him around myself, I tried to pass that on to you. Well, I will be having very strong words with the boy and he won't be staying in Paris. He'll be going back to his mother as soon as possible. I can assure you of that."

This was the result Chrissie wanted but she did feel a tremendous sadness for Monsieur Dupré. "Look, that is your decision, I just ask that you ensure our paths don't cross again, otherwise I will go to the police."

"Of course my dear," he replied, patting her arm gently. "And Chrissie, please be reassured that this will not affect your job here at all."

"I should bloody well hope not," said Josie, incensed. "Chrissie has done nothing wrong."

Once again Monsieur Dupré looked humbled. "Of course you haven't Chrissie. I just wanted to reassure you."

The girls left Monsieur Dupré's office. Some staff had begun to arrive and looked inquisitively at the two girls leaving the boss's office. Chrissie ignored everyone and walked with Josie to reception. "I'll just say that you were here looking for a job," she said to her friend, giving her a hug. "Thanks Josie, it was really good of you to come with me. I'm glad we did that, it was the right thing to do, wasn't it?"

Josie agreed with her friend and left the building heading for the Métro and her own job. She had sent a text to Libby earlier saying that she would be late, and to cover for her. As she headed for the underground station she saw Thierry pulling up in his car outside. She quickly called Chrissie from her mobile to warn her but there was no answer from the office phone or her mobile. Josie was about to head back in when Chrissie emerged from the front door.

"Monsieur Dupré told me to take the day off," she told her friend. "And I'm completely knackered so I'm off home to try and get some sleep."

Josie breathed a sigh of relief. Chrissie hadn't seen Thierry and he hadn't seen her thank goodness.

She reached the office by 9.30 am and fortunately JC hadn't arrived so she was able to explain to Libby what had happened. JC rolled up to the office at 11.00 am, all apologies about the traffic coming back from the countryside on a Monday morning.

Both girls acted as if they were really busy when JC came into the office. They could tell straight away he was in a good mood. He made his way directly to the coffee machine and then sat down on Libby's desk to tell them that he had organised interviews for them both on the Wednesday afternoon at Renseignements. Josie was delighted but Libby seemed less so, concerned about the salary and what the job actually entailed.

"Well, it's up to you to negotiate your own terms and conditions Libby," he said to her grinning. "You will be meeting with one of the Directors, Thomas Frolin. Don't know him myself but Jacques obviously rates him, very up and coming apparently. A bit of a ladies man too I gather."

"Typical of the bloody French," Josie muttered under her breath. JC shot her a look but didn't say anything.

"Muriel will be popping in later, just to see how things work around here," he told them. "Please be so kind as to show her the ropes a bit will you girls, she may be joining us in London."

Once JC had left the room, Libby nearly burst, "Told you, he's lining her up to join him in London, though goodness knows what she can do. I mean, does she do anything? I think he mentioned she was a model but if she is, she's not very busy."

"Well I like her," replied Josie, "I know she doesn't come over as the brightest star in the sky and her taste in men is very dubious. But she's very kind hearted and always smiling and upbeat. I hope it works out for her, it will be tough in London away from her friends and family."

Libby just shook her head. The girls carried on with their usual work routines until lunchtime when Muriel arrived and promptly left with JC. Josie and Libby decided to go out for lunch too and headed for their usual café for a snack. Over lunch Josie remembered that Libby couldn't come with them to the rugby club disco and asked who the visitors were. Libby looked sheepish.

"Well it's Matt," she said.

Josie was surprised. Libby had been so adamant that she wasn't going to resume her relationship with him again especially as Lia seemed to suspect something was going on. Josie secretly thought Libby was more frightened of her father finding out, rather than hurting Lia. Libby explained that Matt had phoned her the week before saying that he couldn't stop thinking about her and was so desperate to see her that he would come over to Paris (which was a first for him). Libby just couldn't resist. She obviously had very strong feelings for him still though unlike Josie who liked to talk about her emotions, Libby tended to bottle them up.

Josie was supportive of Libby saying that she understood and then blurted out to her friend the whole story of her last evening with Max and seeing him with Jane.

"What a pair we are," said Libby, calling the waiter over to their table. "Josie, I think we both need a drink." And she ordered two large glassed of Sancerre, even though they had finished their food. The girls eventually returned to the office 15 minutes late and JC and Muriel were waiting for them.

"You said you'd show Muriel the ropes," he said to them crossly, "where have you been?"

"Out to lunch like you," said Libby boldly, "but we didn't leave until late and we are entitled to a lunch break."

JC was a bit taken aback at Libby's tone but obviously decided to let it go as he had to go out to a meeting and was no doubt feeling guilty about leaving Muriel alone in the office. Once he had left, Muriel sat down in one of the spare office chairs and asked the girls what she could do to help. They didn't really know what to do as they each had their own jobs to get on with and didn't have the time to explain to her the more complex tasks.

"Well you could do some photocopying for me," Libby said to Muriel. The woman looked aghast.

"Photocopying, I don't do photocopying, I am a model. I do phone calls or meet clients…. things like that, that's what JC said."

Josie was struggling to stop herself from laughing but Libby wasn't amused. "Well JC should have explained that it's not like that working in the office. It's about admin and office related tasks, so if you can't do the photocopying, I suggest you wait in his office until he comes back and ask him what you should do."

Both Josie and Muriel were surprised at Libby's outburst. But in her usual way, Muriel just smiled back at Libby as if she didn't have a care in the world.

"Good idea, Libby," she said. "I can phone Maman in Bordeaux and we can have a lovely, long chat."

As soon as Muriel left the office, Libby did not hold back. "What does she think she can do here then? She doesn't have the faintest idea. I blame JC he's put these ideas into her head. She may look good but she's thick as two short planks. Did she think we can make up glamorous jobs for her to do while we slave away at the menial tasks. I am going to have a word with JC, it's just not on."

Josie couldn't help but laugh. She did really like Muriel but understood Libby's view as well. It was a joke expecting her to just walk in and pick things up straight away. And besides, Muriel didn't want to work in the office anyway, that much was obvious.

When JC returned he asked where Muriel was and Libby told him rather curtly that she was on the phone to her mother in his office. A few minutes later, he emerged with Muriel in tow and asked the girls why they hadn't given Muriel anything constructive to do.

"Because there isn't anything constructive we can give her to do," replied Libby, "at least within the job description which you seem to have given her."

Once again that day, both JC and Josie were surprised at Libby's tone. Josie felt she may be pushing their boss too hard, as ridiculous as the situation with Muriel was. JC seemed bewildered. Libby explained that the only non-complicated job she had for Muriel was photocopying but that was turned down. JC looked even more confused. "Muriel can't do photocopying," he replied, "she's a model."

Muriel nodded triumphantly, "this is what I am."

Libby looked exasperated. "Look JC, Muriel can't type, doesn't know how to use a computer, she doesn't speak English and won't photocopy. I don't think she can do book keeping and I'm pretty sure she has no experience of logistics planning, so what exactly do you want her to do here?"

"Don't talk about me as if I am not here," said Muriel.

"Sorry," replied Libby who liked Muriel as a person but also recognised her failings. "It's just we have so much to do with our everyday work and the office move. We just don't have time to show you some basic jobs, even if you were willing to do them."

"OK," said JC who had quickly realised that of course Libby was right and that his expectations of Muriel just slipping into some sort of office role was not going to be realised. Turning to Muriel he told her to pop out and buy herself something new to wear for the dinner they were going to that evening, slipping her a few hundred euros. Her face lit up and she left waving at the girls, saying she'd be back later.

"Right," said JC, once she had left blowing him kisses. "Libby, I think you and I need to have a chat don't you?"

"Oh shit," Libby mouthed to Josie as she followed her boss into his office. Nearly an hour later she emerged wiping her eyes and blowing her nose. JC followed her out and said he was going to catch up with Muriel and wouldn't be back.

"OK, what happened," asked Josie, desperate to know what JC had said to her.

"Well first he wiped the floor with me," replied Libby blowing her nose and drying her eyes, "saying that I was rude to Muriel and him and that I had an attitude problem." Libby was incredulous, "He then told me that he wished he hadn't recommended me to his friend for the job at Renseingements and that he didn't think he could work with me for the office move to London."

Josie was shocked, she couldn't believe their normally reasonably laid back boss, was so upset about this. "So what did you say?"

Libby carried on, "I kept my cool, at first, and said that was fine and that I would hand my notice in today. He was shocked. And then I said I thought I should perhaps take him through everything I did in my normal day to day job, what I had done for the office move and what was still outstanding. I wrote everything down on the white board in his office and his face was a picture. He simply doesn't have a clue what's involved. By this time he had calmed down and was looking very sheepish. I told him that he would have my letter of resignation with a month's notice, according to my contract, on his desk today."

Josie looked aghast, "But Libby…"

"I also advised him that I was still owed three weeks holiday from last year and I have it in writing that he would honour those holidays because, as you know, I was running the whole place practically on my own before you joined, especially in August when everyone buggered off on holiday for a month. I then told him that I would be taking the three weeks as of tomorrow and would return for my final week to complete the books before the financial year end and that in the meantime I hoped that he and Muriel would be able to cope with the extra work which my absence would bring."

"Oh my God, it's a bit drastic don't you think," said Josie, "besides you can't go Libby, how would I manage?"

"I know," replied Libby, "and JC's not stupid. If the office move goes well, then he will get the kudos, not me. He knows that and I know that, but neither of us have acknowledged it openly. Anyway, you've never seen anyone change their mind so quickly in all your life. I just wish you could have seen him grovelling to me, begging me stay, saying that he had been unduly harsh."

Josie couldn't help but laugh at Libby's impersonation of JC, complete with Gallic shrug.

"He then poured his heart out to me about Muriel and his wife and the whole situation. His wife has a lover in London you know which is why she didn't move back to Paris with JC in the first place. He really wants to marry Muriel but his wife, who's Catholic, won't give him a divorce. So he's stuffed basically. His wife knows about Muriel but doesn't openly acknowledge the affair so it's going to be very tricky when he moves back to London, especially as Muriel doesn't really want to go…."

"So, what's happening then?"

"Well, once he'd told me all that, he turned to look at the white board and said that he hadn't realised quite how much work was involved and that he really didn't want me to resign and that he realised he had been an idiot expecting Muriel to be able to help. So he's going to get Madame Vergne to help out more on a day to day basis and I can concentrate on the office move. And we're both getting a pay rise, backdated to October and he's going to really help both of us find other jobs if the one at Renseignements doesn't work out.

"Wow," said Josie, "that's incredible."

"And that's it except that he then asked me if I was happy. That's when I burst into tears and told him all about Matt. He didn't say very much, just came across the room, and put his arms around me. At first I thought he was going to kiss me and I was a bit taken aback but he just said that life and love is hard, no-one prepares us for it and no-one knows what is waiting around the corner. And he told me I should follow my heart."

"If only it was that simple," said Josie sadly.

"On that note, he realised the time and remembered Muriel. So the 'meeting' came to a very abrupt end but I'm glad it all came to a head. I'm not sure what Muriel is going to do but as a gesture I will try to give her some of the more interesting things to do with the office move, like designing the layout, maybe that's something she may be good at. After all, she is a model!"

Both girls started laughing and didn't really get much done for the rest of the day.

At home later, Chrissie was up and making supper for them.

Josie asked how she was and her friend seemed to be OK. "Not looking forward to going back to work tomorrow though," she said. "Thierry has essentially spoilt my relationship with my boss and I'll never forgive him for that. I love this job and don't want to move again."

Chrissie was secretary to the Sales and Marketing Manager at the company which sold high quality apartments throughout France and involved a fair bit of travelling, setting up show apartments and promoting new developments. She had only been working there for 6 months and prior to that had been temping which was both unrewarding and unchallenging.

"Don't worry Chrissie, I am sure Monsieur Dupré is a good man, he won't hold this against you and if he does you would have a good case for unfair dismissal. He's intelligent and experienced enough to know that."

"You're probably right Josie, but I have another problem now. What do I tell Claude? He's rung on my mobile and the land line and left a message asking why I didn't call him last night. So what do I tell him."

"He rang last night too, around 11.30," Josie told her, "asking you to call him whatever time you were back. This is a tricky one. You could tell him the truth but do you know how he will react?"

Chrissie shook her head.

"Or you could forget all about it and just make an excuse."

Josie hesitated, thinking about Chrissie's situation and what she would do if in her shoes.

"To be honest, I would tell him the truth," she said after a few minutes, "lies will only catch you out and if you like him as much as you say you do, Chrissie, then you are going to have to trust him."

Chrissie nodded in agreement but didn't look totally convinced.

"I know," said Josie, "You call him and if he's free and wants to come over, I'll pop over to Libby's for a bit to give you both a bit of space. I don't want to be too late though, didn't get much sleep last night."

"Thanks Josie. That would be great. I know you're right, I'll call Claude and see if he can come over."

Chrissie called Claude who at first was a bit off with her for not calling him the night before but when Chrissie said she needed to explain something to him he agreed to come straight over. Josie gave Libby a quick ring and hurriedly ate her supper. Josie wanted nothing more than to have a bath and climb into bed but her friend needed this time with Claude and it was the least she could do for her.

Just as she was leaving Daniel phoned. Josie explained that she was going over to Libby's as Chrissie was expecting a friend. Daniel caught on straight away. "OK," he said disappointedly, "I just wanted to check Chrissie was OK and how things went at the office, that's all."

Josie promised to call him back when she got to Libby's and explain what had happened. "Why don't I meet you there," he said. Josie agreed to meet him at Libby's and she could tell he was glad, he'd obviously been worrying about Chrissie all day.

Josie explained to Chrissie what was happening and told her friend, "Look, if Daniel brings me home, which he is bound to as really it's you he wants to see. I'm going to invite him in. You can introduce him to Claude and then he'll realise that you're not interested in him other than as a friend. I think it's only fair, Chrissie. We can all get on with our lives without this underlying sensitivity of saying the wrong or right thing to Daniel."

Chrissie was a bit taken aback by Josie's comments and timidly agreed, "But what if Claude has gone by the time you get back, he's working early tomorrow?"

"We won't be late, let's say ten at the latest. Just make sure he's here until then. OK?"

"OK," agreed Chrissie.

Josie felt a bit sorry for her friend who had been through a rough time over the past 24 hours but she also knew it was the right thing to do. It was time to stop giving Daniel false hopes. She understood why Chrissie had called Daniel to come to her rescue the night before. Daniel was that sort of reliable, dependable guy. The guy you could always call in a crisis. But he had feelings too and the sooner he came to terms with the fact that Chrissie did not fancy him, the better.

Just as Josie was leaving the apartment the phone rang. It was Paul. Josie was surprised. He hadn't called her as promised after the New Year party and she thought he just wasn't interested. Paul asked her if she was free for lunch that week and they agreed on the following Thursday. She really liked Paul and if she hadn't been so besotted by Max would probably have taken him up on his previous offers of a date. Unlike Max's dark looks, Paul was tall and fair but well built. He was also an accountant (there were loads of them in that gang) but beyond that Josie didn't know that much about him.

At Libby's, once Daniel arrived they discussed the events of the previous evening and their concerns about Chrissie continuing to work for Monsieur Dupré.

"I hope it's going OK with Claude," said Libby.

Daniel looked a little confused it was obviously the first he had heard of Claude.

"Well we'll soon find out," replied Josie. "It's time for me to go. Thanks Libby and see you tomorrow."

"Give Chrissie my love and tell her to stay strong."

"Can you give me a lift back Dan," said Josie, "you can check on Chrissie and she'll be glad to see you and thank you for last night."

"You'll get to meet Claude too, he's a really nice guy," said Libby.

Daniel looked a little forlorn but then he always looked a bit like that and Josie couldn't tell if he was concerned about Chrissie or miffed that she was seeing someone else.

Back at the flat, Chrissie and Claude were sat at the dining room table, holding hands and gazing into each other's eyes.

"I didn't misjudge him then," thought Josie to herself. "Good, he's just the sort of guy Chrissie needs …. Good looking but a decent guy too."

Following the introduction, Claude said he had to leave due to an early start in the morning and Chrissie went with him to say good night. When she returned, she thanked Daniel again for helping her out and as it looked like he was set to stay for a while, she quite firmly said that everyone needed a good night's rest after the previous evenings high drama. Once he left, Josie asked about Claude's reaction to Chrissie's news.

"He was quite visibly shocked at first," she told Josie. "And then became really angry and wanted me to give him Monsieur Dupré's phone number. I managed to calm him down eventually. The only thing is, we've only known each other a couple of weeks and though I did expect him to be shocked, I didn't expect him to be quite so possessive. Some of the things he said, like 'no-one does that to my woman' and 'I'll get that bastard for trying it on with my girlfriend' put me off a bit, if I'm honest."

"Oh come on Chrissie," said Josie. "How did you expect him to react? He obviously really likes you and you give out the vibes that you like him so you can't blame him for reacting like that. It would have been worse if he hadn't showed he cared."

"I guess you're right," she replied, "but you know how independent I am. I just don't want Claude, or any man come to that, taking over my life."

The girls stayed silent for a moment, each lost in their own thoughts, until Josie broke the silence.

"Caring about you isn't taking over your life Chrissie. Claude's a lovely guy, give him a chance. Just spend time with him and have fun."

Josie's words brought tears to her friend's eyes and she wondered if Chrissie wasn't more upset by the Thierry episode than she was letting on. Josie promised herself she would keep an eye on Chrissie just to make sure.

CHAPTER 8

Tuesday flew by with both Libby and Josie busy at work, the traumas of the previous day forgotten. JC stayed in his office most of the day, popping out for the occasional coffee. During the afternoon he confirmed that they each had an appointment with Thomas Frolin at Renseignements, Libby at 2.30 pm and Josie at 4.00 pm.

Libby was very nonchalant about the whole thing but Josie, who was keener to get herself sorted with a new job, spent the last hour at work checking out the agency's website.

It was an independent agency, run by JC's friend Jacques Fredet, and with three Associate Directors, one of whom was Thomas Frolin. They had an impressive client portfolio of both French and International companies and currently employed 25 staff. Josie didn't have direct experience of PR but had been responsible in her current job for promoting the firm among its key clients so had a vague idea of what was expected. She printed off some information about PR in general to check out later at home. She had learned her lesson with her previous interview and was not going to pretend she was an expert this time. Her aim was to be lively, bubbly, interesting and interested.

Josie spent that evening reading the bumph on PR companies. Claude phoned Chrissie when he arrived home from work and Josie thought her friend was a bit off with him and told her so when she came off the phone.

"I guess I'm still not sure about how possessive he's going to be," she said, "Anyway we're going out at the weekend and a bit of space won't do either of us any harm."

"I guess not," replied Josie who felt that at these early stages of their relationship, having slept together once already they ought to be tearing the clothes of each other at every opportunity. "I guess not everyone is like me though," thought Josie to herself as she climbed into bed, still exhausted from the lack of sleep on Sunday night.

Josie woke early the next morning and took extra time getting ready for the interview. She wore her new green dress, high heel black court shoes and a short waisted black jacket. Fortunately, it wasn't raining but she took a small umbrella just in case in a sleek, slim leather briefcase which her father had given her for Christmas.

At work Libby had made no special effort and was convinced it was all a waste of time.

The morning passed quickly and in no time at all Libby was leaving for her interview. They had originally thought they would go together but there was no-one to man the phones until Madame Vergne came in. She had an appointment during the day but had promised to be back by 3.30 pm. Libby promised to phone Josie to let her know how she got on but by the time Josie left, she hadn't phoned.

In the Métro, Josie re-read the information she had printed off the night before and re-checked her hair and make up for the zillionth time. She had a gut feeling about this interview and the job. The agency sounded a fun and exciting place to work and it also looked like there were genuine opportunities for promotion.

As she came out of the underground station at Sèvres Babylon, Josie continued to have that 'feel good' sensation. The area was on the outskirts of the Latin Quarter and she hadn't been to this part of Paris before. The road leading from the station was full of quaint delis', cheese shops and wine stores, interspersed with chic boutiques and no less than five shoe shops – her passion and weakness. Following the street map, she turned into the rue de la Cherche Midi and found the agency, set back in a colourful courtyard, opposite the famous Parisian bakery, Poilane.

"I may as well go home now," thought Josie. "Shoe shops, clothes shops and the best bakery in Paris, all on the doorstep. Fatal."

She tentatively entered the ground floor offices of

Renseignements and was greeted warmly by a matronly woman on reception. Josie was expecting someone young and haughty, at least that had been her vision of the sort of people who work in PR and advertising. The receptionist told her to take a seat as Monsieur Frolin was running a bit late and offered her a drink. Josie declined as she was so nervous she thought she'd spill it.

A few minutes later she was surprised to see Libby walking across the lobby with one of the most gorgeous looking men she had ever seen. He was a combination of Sasha Distell (very French with a twinkle in his eye) and the French singer from Il Divo. Libby was at her most flirtatious and her face was glowing as she spoke to him. Spotting Josie sitting on the sofa she quickly introduced her.

"Thomas, this is my colleague and friend, Josie. I hope you don't keep her as long as you kept me."

Josie found Libby's flirty manner a bit embarrassing and vowed not to behave like that during the interview. Thomas Frolin shook Libby's hand. He looked as though he was about to kiss it but then thought better of it, thanked her for her time and then turned to Josie. He was even better looking close up, despite some slight wrinkles around his eyes which made him look like he was permanently laughing.

"I shall call you Josephine," he said to her, taking her hand and holding it, she thought, for a fraction too long. Josie had him sussed out straight away – a complete womaniser, 100% certain of his charm. She didn't want to rub him up the wrong way before the interview so she returned his frank gaze and gave a firm handshake (she hated women and men who had weak handshakes but didn't like knuckle crushers either). She followed Thomas Frolin through the lobby and through a large open plan office where three girls were working on computers. There was a radio on low and the atmosphere seemed very relaxed. The girls smiled at Josie as she walked past and she returned their smile. She couldn't help but feel she really liked this place and desperately wanted the job.

They went up a narrow staircase and Thomas opened the door to a large, light airy office on the first floor. He indicated for Josie to sit on one of two low, leather sofas next to the window and offered her a drink, which she again declined.

The interview was relatively informal but nevertheless professional with him asking Josie a number of questions about her experience, her current job, her salary and her career aspirations. Once she had answered all his questions, she had the opportunity to ask him some and was glad that she had researched the company and the PR industry. Hard as it was, she resisted flirting with him as she really wanted to get the job on her own merits and not because of how she looked.

"You are well informed about our agency and the world we operate in," he told her, his eyes wrinkling into a friendly smile. "Tell me, what would make me offer this job to you rather than your colleague?"

Josie thought this was unfair and she wasn't about to slag off Libby to anyone, let alone this man. She thought for a moment and replied.

"From what I've seen and from our conversation, I really feel this is the sort of place I would like to work. Public relations really interests me, it can be so varied. I know it's not all events and glamour, but an element of routine, and the day-to-day stuff is vitally important to ensure a smooth operation. I believe I have a lot to offer, not just in terms of my language and secretarial abilities, but because if you took me on, you would be guaranteed 100% commitment. I'm hungry for this job and would translate that hunger into productivity."

Thomas seemed a bit taken aback by Josie's words but then broke into a smile again. "You know, Josephine, I really like you. It would have been easy for you to say that you want and need this job whilst Libby doesn't. Don't' worry she told me that herself – but you didn't and I admire your loyalty. Libby also told me that you would be a real asset to an agency like ours because of your enthusiasm and boundless energy. I know this may not seem very professional but, subject to your meeting our CEO, Jacques Fredet and with his approval, I would hope to be able to offer you the job."

Josie was delighted and though she knew this showed immediately in her face, she nevertheless tried to maintain an air of sensible dignity.

"That's fantastic, thank you Monsieur Frolin."

"Thomas, please."

"Thomas. But before we go any further, I would like to discuss the terms and conditions."

"Of course," he replied, a smile still lingering in his eyes and he reeled off the salary, working hours, holiday entitlement, and a host of company benefits and provisions. The salary was a little higher than Josie was on currently but there would be no overtime so she would be no worse or no better off. The hours were longer too but she didn't mind that.

As Thomas stood up and held out his hand to Josie, she realised that she liked this man – but didn't fancy him as he was just too perfect. "That's going to make life easier," she thought, "I don't know if I could work for someone I really fancied."

He led her back to the reception area and asked the receptionist, Claire, to take down her personal details so they could get back in touch to arrange a meeting with Monsieur Fredet.

"Thank you once again Thomas," she said shaking his hand. "I really do appreciate the offer and believe me you won't regret it."

"I am sure I won't Josephine," he replied. "We'll be in touch."

Leaving the courtyard and heading for the Métro, Josie was grinning from ear to ear. She really didn't expect to be offered the job there and then and she would be eternally grateful to Libby for boosting her up so much. She immediately called her friend from her mobile and Libby answered after just one ring.

"Well, how did you get on? Wasn't he divine?"

"He offered me the job, Libby, and all thanks to you."

"Fabulous, I hope you accepted. What do you mean thanks to me?"

Josie explained what Thomas had said and Libby just laughed.

"To be honest, it was tempting as the offices and the area are so lovely but I would never be able to work for a dish like that, wow," drooled Libby. "He was just too good looking and sexy. I'd be a nervous wreck all the time, checking that I looked good. Anyway I really think that with your personality you'd be very suited to Public Relations. Whereas I am just a boring number cruncher and intend remaining so."

"Well we have to celebrate, but only when it's all signed, sealed and delivered. I have to meet Jacques Fredet first before I get a proper offer."

"I gather from JC he is an absolute puppy dog, so don't worry. We'll celebrate when you get an offer in writing," said Libby, "provided it doesn't clash with Matt's visit."

Matt was due to come over the last weekend in January and

Josie hoped that she would have a firm job offer from Renseignements by then.

When she arrived home Chrissie was waiting to hear about the interview and was delighted with Josie's news.

"How was your day Chrissie?" Josie asked, thinking that it may have been awkward.

"Actually it was fine," her friend replied. "Monsieur Dupré called me into his office and told me that he had spoken to Thierry. Thierry apparently denied everything but his father stood his ground and sent him back to Rennes to his mother. I don't know what that means for his studies and quite frankly I don't care."

"Good riddance to the little shit," spat Josie.

"Monsieur Dupré told me that I wasn't to worry about my job or anyone else finding out what happened. It's to be strictly between us and if ever he can do anything to help me or to make up for what happened to let him know. He also asked me if I could let this be 'water under the bridge' and that neither of us need ever refer to it again."

"Well, that's good to hear Chrissie."

"He looked so forlorn, almost broken. So I said of course I would and that I hoped this wouldn't jeopardise our working relationship. Monsieur Dupré said that it categorically wouldn't and I do believe him. I think we may be a bit uncomfortable with each other for a while but hopefully that will pass. It does help that I don't work for him directly so with any luck everything will calm down now…. I still can't believe this all happened only last Sunday. It feels like a lifetime ago."

Josie agreed with her and although the job offer from Renseignements was not yet official, they celebrated with a bottle of champagne from the local deli.

The next day in the office, JC phoned from his meeting in Lyons to find out how the girls had got on. He was delighted to hear Josie's news.

She later found out that JC had given her a glowing reference, but had not been so forthcoming about Libby. Ever the sceptic, she believed this was essentially because he needed Libby to run his life, the office and plan the move to London. But she did feel good knowing that he valued her too.

Josie left early for lunch to meet Paul at the Place de l'Opéra which was equidistant from their respective offices. They met in the Café de la Paix. Josie watched Paul walking across the restaurant to join her. She couldn't help but think how attractive he was. After exchanging normal chit-chat and ordering lunch, Paul thanked Josie for meeting him as he had something he wanted to ask her.

"Sure, fire away," she said.

"Well, the day after the New Year's Eve bash, Max phoned me. He was obviously fishing for something but I wasn't sure what until he asked me if you stayed over. I told him that you hadn't and basically, he warned me off you. Told me you were a tease and that I'd be wasting my time. I told him to mind his own business but he still told me to be careful. I found the conversation quite bizarre as normally Max is the one to goad us all on …. I think he gets a kick out of it as he and Anna have been together so very long. But I still couldn't get my head around it. I really like you Josie and I don't think you're a tease at all. So I was wondering if you would know why Max would warn me off? Is there something I should know?"

"He knows," thought Josie to herself. "But how much does he know?" She couldn't believe that Max would bad mouth her like that to Paul. She realised that it was probably because he wanted to keep her to himself but still she felt betrayed.

Their lunch arrived so Josie had a few minutes to gather her thoughts. She could claim absolute disbelief but was sure that Paul would not buy that or she could come clean. She didn't know if he knew more than he was letting on and so decided to try and find out before admitting anything.

Looking him straight in the eye, Josie asked him, "He's your friend Paul, why do you think he would warn you off?"

Paul seemed taken aback. He was obviously expecting her to either deny or admit to something. He thought carefully for a moment and said, "I think you're having an affair with him. I've known Max for a long time and he can be a lady killer. I thought he had finally settled down with Anna but I guess he's up to his old tricks again. Am I right?"

The look of guilt which spread across Josie's face told it all.

"I am right, aren't I?" said Paul again.

Josie nodded in acknowledgement.

Paul reached over and took her hand. "Look, I'm not blaming you. I know what Max is like and I've had more than one broken heart crying on my shoulder before, including my own ex-girlfriend. So don't look like that Josie, honestly I really do understand."

Josie thought she was going to cry and wiped a suspect tear away with the back of her hand. Paul passed her a napkin.

"Thanks," she said, wiping her eyes and nose. "You are right Paul. But it's completely over with now and has been since ….. Well since last Thursday actually." And she told him the whole story, about meeting at Longchamps, the regular Monday evenings around his flat, his comments about being comfortable with Anna and her suspicions about Jane.

"I think your suspicions about Jane are unfounded," Paul told her. "Max and Jane have been organising a surprise birthday party for Anna – it's this Saturday actually. And anyway, Jane is really besotted with her new guy apparently. He's incredibly wealthy and a good looking chap which suit's Jane right down to the ground, she's very materialistic."

"Well Max and Jane looked very intimate the last time I saw them together," Josie replied, still convinced there was something going on. Although knowing they had been organising a party for Anna strangely made her feel a bit better.

"I was going to invite you to go to Anna's party with me Josie. But I guess under the circumstances…," he trailed off.

Josie didn't know what to say. She would love to go to the party with Paul just to piss Max off, especially as he had warned Paul to leave her alone. But she didn't know if she could cope with Max and Anna or Max and Jane or Max and anyone else come to that.

"Well, I guess you wouldn't want to invite me now anyway," she said to Paul.

"Quite the opposite actually," he replied. "I think it would be good for you and it would show Max that you are 'over' him – you are over him aren't you Josie?"

Josie nodded, a little too quickly because she wasn't entirely sure if she was over Max.

"And it would also show him that he can't control people's lives, yours and mine especially," Paul added. "So what do you think?"

"I don't know Paul," she replied. "I am over Max but it is still very raw, particularly with what you've just told me. If I do go, it would be for all the wrong reasons and that's not fair on you."

"Fair enough but if you change your mind, let me know. I'm not planning on inviting anyone else so call me before Saturday either way."

They finished their food quickly, both lost in their respective thoughts. Paul paid the bill despite Josie's protestations and as they left the restaurant, he again asked her to think about going to the party with him, to prove a point if nothing else. Josie said that she would think about it and gave him a peck on the cheek, "Thanks Paul, not just for lunch but for telling me about Max. It hurts to know that he said those terrible things about me. But in a way I'm glad as it just confirms that he actually is the selfish, two-timing bastard I thought he was."

Paul pulled Josie to him and wrapped her up in a big bear hug. "As I said before, I really like you Josie and would love to get to know you better. There's no rush but even if you don't come to the party with me, perhaps we can go out and have lunch again. Take it slowly?"

"That would be lovely Paul and I will call you before Saturday but I'm still not sure what to do."

"I'm not going to force you but I honestly do think it would do you the world of good, and it would certainly give me great pleasure. Take care and I'll speak to you soon."

As Josie walked away from the restaurant she turned to look back and caught Paul gazing after her intently. She waved at him and he threw her a kiss back. She couldn't help but smile and had butterflies in her stomach. "Perhaps he's right," she thought, "I should go with him to the party. It would be worth it just to see the look on Max's face."

Back at the office she told Libby all about the conversation with Paul and the invitation to the party.

"You should definitely go," said Libby. "Max has no right to interfere in your life like that. Paul is such a sensible, balanced guy and he's quite good looking too. Anyway I'm going. Daniel phoned while you were out and invited us to go with him – general invitation from Max apparently. So if the going gets tough I'll be there for you."

"Well in that case I'll definitely go, but with Paul not you and Daniel. What about Chrissie?"

"She's going out with Claude that night. Daniel phoned her first. I'll bet he only asked her to go initially and when she turned him down..."

Josie laughed. "We were sloppy seconds. Dan will never learn. He's met Claude and must realise he can't compete. Still you have to admire him for his determination."

Josie decided to call Paul the next day as she wanted him to think she had given the invitation careful thought. She also booked a hair appointment, waxing session and sun bed. She was going to look fabulous and starve herself until the party so her stomach would be nice and flat.

Just as they were wrapping up for the day, Josie's phone rang. It was Claire the receptionist from Renseignements asking if she could come and meet Jaques Fredet on Tuesday at 9.00 am. Josie confirmed that she could and let out a whoop when she hung up.

"I'm meeting the big boss of Renseignements on Tuesday," she told Libby. "Hopefully things will move pretty fast afterward and I'll be able to start in a month or so."

"What about me and this place," replied Libby, "what are we going to do without you?"

"Muriel," they both said together and burst out laughing. At that point Muriel walked into the office to meet JC, which only made them laugh even more. Muriel walked past them shaking her head as if to say, "mad crazy English girls!"

At home that evening Josie told Chrissie about lunch with Paul and her decision to go to the party.

"I wish I was coming now," Chrissie said, "but I've already promised Claude we'd go out and he's working every night this week so I don't want to let him down. I'd love to see the look on Max's face when you arrive with Paul. Maybe I'll cancel my date with Claude, just to see that."

Josie knew her friend was joking and told her not to dare cancel her date.

Later that evening the girls had a 'trying on' session ready for the party and Josie eventually decided on a pair of tight jeans and off the shoulder cream blouse that was very flattering to her figure. She added a loose gold belt and a pair of dangly, gold earrings that practically reached down to her shoulders. The final touch was 12 slim gold bangles that jangled with every movement, putting Josie immediately in the party mood.

She also took Chrissie up on her offer to borrow her high

heeled cream boots. Paul was so tall they would give her a bit more height. "Better for smooching," she said as she admired her appearance in the mirror and there's going to be plenty of that."

The next day she phoned Paul and told him she would go to the party. She didn't say that Libby was going with Dan, she'd tell him that on the night, in case he thought that had influenced her decision. He seemed delighted and arranged to pick her up at 8.00 pm from the flat. Josie offered to meet him at the rugby and cricket club. But he insisted on picking her up as he also lived in central Paris.

Josie realised that she had no idea where he lived and in fact knew very little about him at all. "Plenty of time to find out on Saturday," she said to herself as she hung up.

With all the arrangements in place the three girls spent Saturday attending a whirl of numerous appointments to make themselves look good. After a long soak in the bath, Josie finally put on her make up and dressed in her chosen outfit.

"See you later," Josie shouted to Chrissie, "as Paul buzzed the intercom. "I'll be right down Paul."

Chrissie was a bit fed up that she wasn't going to the party and popped into the hallway to see Josie off.

"You look stunning Josie."

"Thanks Chrissie, you too," said Jose rummaging through her handbag to check she had her keys.

"I really wish I was coming now."

"Well it's not too late. I'm sure you and Claude could come along, Paul will give you a lift."

"It wouldn't be fair on Claude," Chrissie replied, "he won't know anyone and anyway the place is so very British and full of English people, he would feel a bit left out. It's very cliquey there don't you think?"

"Yes I do," said Josie, "and I would never dream of joining… very all England and all that! But it's a good laugh sometimes and hopefully tonight will be one of those times."

Paul was waiting on the pavement for Josie. He looked very attractive in cream chinos and a light blue linen shirt that highlighted his eyes. He opened the door of his car for Josie and she noted his admiring glances as she slipped into the passenger seat.

The drive to the rugby and cricket club took around half an

hour and Josie used the time to ask Paul about himself. He told her that he lived in 13th arrondissement, near the Jardins de Luxembourg. He'd been working in Paris for two years and though he loved it, long term he hoped to transfer to the United States. His speciality was corporate taxation and he wanted to get a good all round experience before moving onwards and upwards. Paul was from Guildford in Surrey and had an older brother and sister. His father was 'something in the city' and his mother a housewife. From what Josie picked up he obviously came from a pretty well off background.

Paul also told her he really enjoyed playing most sports, especially squash and cricket. But that his rugby days were over due to a longstanding knee injury from University.

Josie felt very comfortable with him and enjoyed listening to him talk about himself. Paul had a charming self-deprecating manner that showed he didn't take himself too seriously. All in all, he seemed ideal for her but she couldn't help thinking about Max and the passion she had felt for him from that first moment they met. She didn't feel the same way about Paul. "Maybe that will come with time," she said to herself.

Once they arrived at the club, Paul, a true gentleman, helped Josie out of the car, giving her a big smile as if he understood how nervous she was at the prospect of seeing Max again.

"You look sensational," he told her, giving her a peck on the cheek, "I'm so proud to have you as my date."

Josie smiled at him and then froze. Standing on the first floor veranda of the club was Max, staring down at them with a thunderous look on his face. She quickly recovered, taking Paul's arm, and ignoring Max completely. Josie walked with Paul into the club laughing and joking as they went in.

Josie couldn't believe how much had happened since New Year's Eve just a couple of weeks ago. Libby and Daniel were hanging around the doorway looking out for her. Paul headed for the bar with Dan to get them drinks and Libby pulled Josie into a corner by the door.

"Max made a bee-line straight for us when we came in," Libby told her, "and asked where the rest of the gang was, obviously fishing about you. So I told him that Chrissie wasn't coming and that you were coming later with Paul. You should have seen his face. Anyway since then he's been in and out to the veranda every ten seconds or so. Anna is getting pretty fed up with him and they've had words. It's just been so funny to watch him."

"He clocked us arriving," said Josie, "and Paul was being really touchy feely. Max had a face like thunder. I wonder if he'll say anything."

Paul and Daniel returned with drinks and some of their cricketing gang in tow. The table was situated close to the veranda. Josie had her back to the patio doors and Paul sat next to her with his arm draped casually over the back of her chair. She couldn't see Max from where she was sitting but sensed that he was watching her.

When Paul left their table to chat to another couple, Libby leaned over from her place opposite. "Max hasn't stopped staring at you," she whispered quickly before Paul came back to the table. Josie couldn't resist and sneaked a look. Max caught her eye and stared piercingly at her. She turned back to speak to Libby as if she hadn't seen him but realised that her hands were shaking. "Pull yourself together girl," she told herself sternly, "he is an out and out shit and you are over him!"

She hated the fact that Max still made her stomach lurch and her heart beat faster and willed Paul to come back to the table so she could concentrate her attentions on him.

The evening passed very pleasantly with good company, excellent food and a lively atmosphere. Anna came over to their table and thanked Paul for the gift from him and Josie. Josie was surprised, she hadn't realised that Paul had put her name with his. When she had asked him what to do about a card and present, he had told her that he would take care of it. "I didn't realise you two were an item," she commented, giving Josie a rather haughty look as if she wasn't quite good enough for Paul.

Both women looked each other up and down, appraising outfits. Josie knew that she looked great, particularly when she assessed Anna's own appearance. Their host was wearing a simple, plain black midi length dress with low heeled court shoes and pearl stud earrings. Her frizzy, mousy hair was tied back behind her ears with cheap, plastic clips.

Josie pulled back her shoulders, pushed out her boobs and sucked in her tummy. Anna lifted a quizzical eyebrow, her disapproval evident.

"Well you don't know all my secrets, Anna," replied Paul

standing up and giving her a kiss on the cheek, "happy birthday. Max has done you proud."

"Humph," she replied. "He's been like a bear with a sore head all evening. I don't know what's got into him."

"That's unlike Max," said Paul.

"I let it out accidentally that I knew about the party. Apparently Max and Jane had wanted it to be such a big surprise. But it's impossible to keep these things a complete secret and I think that's really cheesed him off."

Josie and Libby looked at each other. Libby burst out laughing drawing the attention of Paul and Anna. She pushed Daniel, almost out of his chair, to cover her embarrassment, "Oh Daniel, you are a card, that's the best joke I've heard all year."

Daniel looked completely mystified at her behaviour which almost set Josie off laughing.

"Where is Max anyway?" asked Paul. "I haven't seen him all evening."

"Out on the veranda again I suppose. He seems to have spent most of the evening out there, goodness knows why, its bloody freezing. If I didn't know any better I'd think he was waiting for someone," commented Anna, moving to the next table to thank her guests for their presents. The girls could barely look at each other.

"What the hell's got into you two," said Daniel, "we better scale back on the drinks, pace ourselves."

As Paul sat down he whispered in Josie's ear, "I think Max is avoiding us, don't you. I know he saw us arrive. Are you OK?"

Josie nodded.

"Come on let's dance," said Libby and the group joined the others gyrating on the dance floor to Culture Club's Karma Chameleon. Paul was a good dancer and began to jive with Josie flinging her all around the room. After a few more dances, Josie and Paul headed back to the table. "I'm boiling," Paul said leading her out onto the veranda, "let's pop out for a second."

He grabbed her hand and pulled her after him. The night air was cold and Paul put his arms around Josie and drew her to him. He held her like that for a few seconds and then bent his head to kiss her. His kisses were tender and slow at first and then more demanding, with his tongue circling her lips and then moving down to her neck. Josie returned his kisses with a hungry passion. Paul was releasing all the pent up anger she felt inside for Max.

"Lovely," Paul said as he tore himself away from her kisses and pulled her close. It felt good being held tenderly by someone who was obviously into her in a big way. His kisses had turned her on but this time she wasn't going to rush into bed with Paul, she wanted to take things slowly.

"Come on, let's get back in," Paul said, releasing her from his arms and taking her hand, "it's bloody freezing out here."

"Looked pretty damn hot to me," said a voice from the opposite end of the balcony. It was Max.
"Sorry Max we didn't see you there," said Paul smiling. "What are you doing out here, its bloody nobbling? Anna has been looking for you all evening." The two men held each other's gaze. "Come on Josie, let's get another drink. See you later Max."

Paul pulled Josie into the room behind him and then with his arm at the base of her back, guided her towards the bar. "Sorry about that Josie, I really didn't know he was out there. I hope that wasn't too awkward for you?"

Josie didn't buy it. She had the feeling Paul knew exactly what he was doing but she didn't object. She had really enjoyed kissing him and at the same time showing Max that she was over him. Although why she felt so guilty she didn't know.

"I think you knew exactly what you were doing, Paul Stevenson," she told him smiling.

A few minutes later Max stormed back into the room, glaring at Paul and Josie. Paul went to get more drinks and Josie sat down at their table. She was in a complete daydream, thinking about Paul and what a really great guy he was and she didn't see Max sit next to her.

"Enjoying yourself are you Josie?" he asked in a low, almost threatening tone.

Josie nearly jumped out of her skin. "Oh God Max, I didn't see you there. Sorry. Yes, it's a great party. Well done to you and Jane for organising it."

"What do you think you're playing at?" he practically growled at her. "What's this with Paul, I didn't even realise you knew him."

"There's a lot you don't know about me Max. And what I do with my life and whom I choose to see is my business not yours," she replied. She stood up, picked up her handbag and made for the toilet. Max grabbed her arm. "Don't fuck with me Josie, you'll regret it."

"I already do!" she replied and walked away head held high. She passed Paul on his way back to the table. "Won't be a moment," she said and headed for the ladies.

When Paul reached the table, Max was still sitting there.

"Great party Max," said Paul. "This must have cost a bob or two. I hope Anna appreciates it."

"What's with you and Josie then," Max replied ignoring Paul's comments, "I thought she wasn't your type."

"No Max, she is definitely my type, it was you who thought she wasn't. I wonder why that is?"

"Have you slept with her?"

"Max. That's our business not yours. Why are you so interested?"

"Just wondering that's all. I told you before, Josie is a real tease, don't want to see you wasting your time."

"No time with Josie is wasted, believe you me," replied Paul, knowing that this would make Max assume they had slept together. "And I can positively assure you she is not a tease."

Paul felt a bit guilty as it sounded as though he knew Josie better than he really did, but he didn't want Max to have the upper hand.

"Here she comes now," added Paul as Josie approached the table. She was surprised and intrigued to see the two men talking and looked expectantly at Paul.

"We were just talking about you," he said, giving her a peck on the cheek, which Josie thought was a bit OTT given she had only been gone a few minutes.

"Really," she replied looking directly at Max. "Anything you'd like to share with me?"

"Must mingle," he replied avoiding her eyes, "Anna will be wondering where I've got to. Catch you later."

"Well?" said Josie as Max left the table.

"Max warned me off you again Josie. He seems really angry. I led him to believe that we knew each other quite well actually. I hope you don't mind?" Paul looked sheepish, "He was really winding me up."

"Don't worry Paul, so did I. Max came and sat next to me just after you left and was quite stroppy about us. I told him basically to mind his own business."

"Good, I'm glad," said Paul, "he's acting like a prize idiot throwing his toys out of the pram."

As Libby and Dan sat down at the table, the DJ announced that Max would like to say a few words. As he stood on the small platform that served as a stage, Josie couldn't help but admire his dark, brooding good looks. He was wearing navy chinos and a white shirt. His dark blue eyes sparkled in his handsome face. Josie wasn't sure if it was his enjoyment at having a captive audience or too much alcohol. Either way he looked good enough to eat. Anna standing next to him on the other hand looked plain and dowdy, in a black, low cut midi length dress that did nothing for her fair complexion and frizzy mousy hair. It also showed her complete lack of cleavage.

Max launched into a speech thanking everyone for coming. Paul put his arm around Josie and whispered, "Let's go after the speeches. I know this lovely little club off the Rue Mouffetard which stays open all night and serves the best coffee in Paris. I want you to myself for a while this evening, if that's OK?"

"That would be lovely," she replied, grateful that Paul didn't suggest going back to his place.

Max finished his short speech by asking all the guests to raise their glasses to Anna and to wish her happy birthday.

"It's more like a bloody wedding than a birthday party," commented Libby as they 'toasted' Anna.

Anna thanked everyone and the DJ played a romantic number while Max and Anna danced.

"Oh dear," said Libby as she watched the couple twirl uncomfortably around the dance floor, "hardly loves young dream."

Josie watched the couple closely. There seemed to be no tenderness or sexual chemistry between them. In fact, they acted more like a couple forced into an uncomfortable dance at their fiftieth wedding anniversary.

Max caught Josie's eye and glared, thunder clouds crackling. She turned away embarrassed that he'd caught her watching them so intently.

Paul and Josie said their goodbye's and headed for the door. Josie looked around and again caught Max staring after them. She just couldn't help herself and winked at him knowingly as Paul led her out of the building by her hand.

Ellis Rose

CHAPTER 9

As they headed for Rue Mouffetard in Paul's car, both were quiet, lost in their own thoughts. Josie stared out of the window as the countryside soon turned to buildings and became the city. When they were half way there, Josie's mobile beeped to indicate she had a message. It was from Max.

"Who's texting you at this time of night," Paul asked her.

She didn't want to admit it was Max until she had read what it said. "Oh it's Chrissie," she replied opening the message, "says she won't be home tonight, surprise, surprise."

In fact the message from Max said, "Can't stop thinking about you. Don't make a mistake."

Very cryptic thought Josie glad she hadn't told Paul the text was from Max. They arrived at the Club. Josie thought the front door looked like the entrance to someone's house. Paul paid at the desk for a private room.

"I know this may seem a bit odd but it's really different in here," he told her, "very selective."

They were escorted to a room which contained a pair of low, comfortable sofas, a coffee table with steaming coffee and a glorious choice of petits fours. There was a large TV screen in the corner and a low cupboard displaying a series of books with no visible writing on the spine. Josie thought the place was very odd but decided to trust Paul's judgement.

The woman who had escorted them to their room smiled and before leaving, she indicated a buzzer to ring if they needed anything.

"What is this place," Josie asked Paul as they sat down. Paul poured them each a coffee and replied, "It's a real gem. I guess once upon a time it was a sort of club for men who valued privacy, if you know what I mean but the owner, an American woman in fact, recognised the need for a place for couples to go undisturbed. I think it's aimed at couples who are having affaires, it's very private and intimate, don't you think?" he said smiling.

"I suppose so. Why the television though?"

"It's not just for porn, if that's what you're thinking. To be honest, the guys and I come here from time to time to watch sports. We get superb service. There's an à la carte menu and the drinks are cheaper than most bars. More importantly you don't get a lot of drunken French men hanging around, and challenging you to prove their virility."

"Quite bizarre," said Josie, reaching for her third petit fours. "Porn and sport what a heady mix. These are delicious by the way."

"So are you," said Paul, leaning over and kissing her on the mouth. "You taste lovely too."

Josie moved closer to him and put her arms around his neck, drawing his face towards hers. She kissed him deeply on the mouth, opening his lips with her probing tongue.

They spent the next half an hour just kissing each other like a couple of teenagers on a first date. When Paul eventually pulled away, he looked her directly in the eyes and said, "You're really lovely Josie and if we carry on like this I won't be responsible for my actions, so drink your coffee and I'll order some fresh."

Again Josie was touched by his thoughtfulness, particularly as she had felt a bit uncomfortable in this strange place. Paul had totally put her at ease and she felt very relaxed, safe and comfortable with him.

They sat together on the sofa chatting easily with an occasional 'snog' in between until Josie started to feel her eyes closing. "I'm really tired now Paul," she said, laying her head against his shoulder. "I think it's time to go home."

"Well it is 6 am," he told her checking his Breitling Navitimer.

"Really, gosh the time has flown. That's what happens in such good company."

She smiled and kissed him again. Paul stood and helped Josie to her feet. He wrapped her tightly in his arms and told her she was very special and he would like to see her again.

"I'd love to Paul," she said hugging him. So they arranged to meet that afternoon to go for a walk in the Jardins de Versailles.

At home, Josie was so tired she just dropped her clothes on the floor, crawled naked into bed, not waking until noon the next day when the telephone rang. She heard Chrissie answer the phone and say, "Sorry Max, not sure where she is at the moment. Can I get her to call you? Sure, will do. Bye!"

Chrissie stuck her head around the door. "Did you hear that?" she asked her friend.

"Sure did, what did he say?"

"He said he'd tried your mobile but it was switched off and wondered if you could call him on his mobile as soon as possible."

Josie reached into her handbag and pulled out her mobile which indeed was switched off from the night before. Switching it on there were several text messages from Paul, Libby, Max and voicemail. Voicemail informed her she had three new messages. The one message from Max asked her to call him as soon as possible. The others were both from Paul at different times throughout the morning asking her to call him too.

Josie didn't know what to do. If she ignored Max's calls, knowing him he would persist until he got hold of her but she didn't want him to think she wanted to speak to him. On the other hand, she was intrigued to hear what he had to say.

"I'm going to call him Chrissie, stay here and you can listen in."

She dialled Max's mobile and he picked it up on the first ring.

"Josie, where have you been I've been calling you all morning."

"I've been sleeping," she told him, "I didn't get in until 6 this morning."

"Stayed at Paul's did you?" asked Max harshly. There was a long pause and she could practically feel Max smouldering down the phone and ready to launch into an angry rant.

"It's none of your business Max. What do you want anyway?"

"Look Josie, I'm really sorry about the other week and what I said. I never meant to imply that you were anything other than important to me. Seeing you with Paul last night made me realise how much I miss you and how much I want you. Will you come over tomorrow evening?"

Josie couldn't believe her ears. Did this guy really think she was that shallow and prepared to hop straight back into bed with him at the drop of a hat?

"Josie we really need to talk, you mean so much to me…"

"Sorry Max but I'm not interested," she replied. "I deserve better than a fuck once a week while your girlfriend is away. It's taken me a while to realise it but you are just using me and I'm not prepared to be used any more."

"I know it may seem like that Josie, but I really do care for you, I can't get you out of my mind. I can't bear the thought of you with Paul……," he trailed off.

"Well you better get used to the idea Max because I really like Paul and I'm seeing him again this afternoon. I'm not interested in a secret relationship which involves you fucking my brains out once a week…"

"I thought we fucked each other's brains out Josie," he said huskily, "come on you have to admit we have something special going on here."

Josie wavered and felt stirrings in her groin that were beyond her control.

"I am not interested in going to bed with you once a week and being rewarded with a meal and a bottle of wine. I deserve more than that."

"You do deserve more, a lot more," he said, "but I've explained the situation with Anna…"

Josie cut him off sharply, her temper rising. "All you've explained Max is that you are comfortable with her and if that's what you want out of a relationship then fine. Just leave me alone to get on with my own life and you get on with yours. I will say one thing though, if I had to make a choice between comfortable and safe versus passionate and exciting, I know which I would choose." Max was silent at the other end of the phone but Josie could hear him breathing. "That's all I have to say really Max. So please don't keep calling me, there's nothing to gain in it, believe me."

"You know you want me Josie. I could see it in your eyes last night. This isn't the end and you know it. I will have you again, trust me, and you can take that to the bank." Max hesitated as if considering whether to say more. "Just be careful of Paul, he's not as straightforward as you may think. There's a bit more going on there…Just be careful." And he hung up.

Josie wasn't sure who had the upper hand in the conversation, though Max definitely had the final word.

"Oh my," said Chrissie fanning herself, "you've certainly rattled his cage."

"Do you think so?" Josie replied, still thinking about the conversation with Max and his comment about Paul.

Josie decided not to mention anything to Paul when they met later that day. The couple spent a relaxing afternoon strolling around the beautiful gardens and lakes which surrounded the Palace of Versailles. The place was virtually empty as it was still January but it was very pleasant. They stopped for a snack on the way home and when he dropped Josie off, Paul told her he would call her in the week. Josie hoped he would as she was really getting to like Paul. Although she realised an element of her liking him was because it pissed Max off so much.

The following weekend was the rugby club dance. Claude was on shift all weekend so Chrissie had decided to go with Daniel.

"Are you going to the dance with Paul?" she asked Josie.

"He hasn't mentioned it," she replied, "but don't worry, I'll come with you and Daniel. I won't leave you spend the evening with him."

"Daniel's not that bad," tutted Chrissie.

"OK, I'll leave you two lovebirds alone then," she said slyly.

"You will not," laughed Chrissie, "but seriously I'd really appreciate you coming with me and Dan. I think that makes it kind of clear we aren't 'going together', if you get my drift? I really don't want to lead him on."

"I would have thought it's a bit too late for that," said Josie, "poor Dan just refuses to give up."

"Well I've been pretty clear about my relationship with Claude. I really don't know what else I'm meant to do."

CHAPTER 10

The following Tuesday, Josie had her meeting with Jacques Fredet at Renseignements. When she emerged from the Métro, she was instantly impressed yet again by that area of Paris. The receptionist, Claire, was as pleasant as ever and this time Josie was less nervous and did accept a cup of coffee.

Within a few minutes, Monsieur Fredet, appeared and gave Josie a very warm welcome to the agency. "My old friend, JC and Thomas, both speak very highly of you young lady," he said in English as they walked up the stairs towards his office. "I was very much looking forward to meeting you today."

Josie liked the man immediately. He was tall and broad with a shock of very white hair and friendly brown eyes. His English was impeccable and his accent barely traceable.

The office was stunning, a huge light room with two French windows which opened onto small balconies overlooking the courtyard. The décor was light and airy. At the far end of the room was what looked like an antique desk and nearer the door, a series of cream, leather sofas surrounding a glass table. "Wow," Josie couldn't help herself. The office was superb.

"Perks of the job," he said indicating that she should sit down on one of the sofas. He sat opposite her and then switched to French. Josie guessed he was testing her language skills and so replied easily to his questions about herself and her experience in France. Jacques Fredet outlined the history of the agency and his plans for expansion in the future.

"Our future is across all of Europe, not just in France. So anyone with additional languages will be of great benefit."

Josie told him that she spoke Italian too and that she had a good understanding of Spanish, a language she would like to perfect. They continued chatting for about half an hour and finally he stood up and held out his hand.

"Well Josie, you seem to have all the qualities we require for the post. I think you will fit in very well. Welcome to Renseignements. I'll speak with Thomas later today and we'll get an official job offer to you this week along with the terms and conditions... I do hope you will accept and join the team?"

"Thank you, Monsieur Fredet," she replied shaking his hand vigorously, 'I would be delighted to work here with you." She was beaming, the agency, the people all seemed just perfect.

"Excellent, I'll get Claire to introduce you to everyone now if you have time?" he asked her.

"No time like the present," she said, nodding her head enthusiastically. Back downstairs, he said goodbye, repeating that he looked forward to having her working for the agency. Claire then took Josie around the offices introducing her to the secretaries, the accountants, book keepers, the account executives and the other two directors, Jean Paul Benet and Phillippe McKay. They were all very pleasant and welcomed Josie to the agency.

Heading back to the office she switched on her mobile to call the girls to tell them the good news. There was a message from Paul asking how the interview went and to give him a call. She called him back immediately.

"I've got the job," she told him excitedly. "I'm just waiting for the official offer letter and I can hand in my notice to JC."

"Well done Josie, that's my gal'. Great news," he replied, "do you fancy celebrating with me tonight?"

"I'd love too," she replied.

They made arrangements for that evening and then Josie phoned Chrissie. She was delighted as was Libby, JC and the Madames' when she told them her news back at the office.

"We'll have to sort a leaving date for you Josie," JC told her. "It may be that we do something on a transitional basis as we won't replace you over here, we'll recruit someone in London."

"That's fine," replied Josie, "I am sure Renseignements will understand - Particularly as your old friend is the big boss JC."

"Less of the old, young lady," JC said laughing. "I think this call's for a celebration. Ladies, lunch is on me. We'll shut the office for a few hours and sod the Americans."

Josie and Libby loved it when JC was in this sort of mood, magnanimous and full of generosity. Lunch would be at his favourite bistro just around the corner and would include a good few glasses of wine. Josie's day was just getting better and better.

Lunch extended over two hours and neither Josie nor Libby was capable of much work that afternoon. They did the bare minimum until 5pm when they both left the office, Josie looking forward to her date with Paul and Libby to clean her flat ahead of Matt's visit. He was due Friday lunchtime and she had booked the day off so she could meet him at the airport.

"I can't wait to see him again, Josie," Libby said. "I know it's wrong as he's married and all that but it's like part of me is missing when we aren't together. Do you know what I mean?"

Josie wasn't sure she did. In her past relationships and the affaire with Max she hadn't ever felt like that. With Max particularly, as she had known the situation early on she had never really expected more than he had to offer, despite wanting more. She hoped one day she would feel like that about a guy and who knows, that could be Paul, she thought to herself as she headed home.

Chrissie was also home ahead of her and had a bottle of champagne on ice waiting. "I thought we'd celebrate by eating out tonight," Chrissie said as she poured a glass for Josie.

"Shit, I've arranged to go out with Paul tonight, sorry."

"That's OK," Chrissie replied jokingly, "I know when I'm not wanted."

"Sorry Chrissie. Thanks for the champagne, it's a lovely gesture."

Chrissie decided that she would enjoy an evening in with a long soak in the bath and catch up on personal emails. Josie looked at her watch and realised the time. Paul was due to pick her up in 15 minutes and she hadn't even showered yet. She was also feeling quite tipsy from the wine at lunch time, topped up with the champagne. She tried Paul's mobile but it was switched off. Josie hopped into the shower and let the hot water pound onto her head in the hope it would clear it. She was just drying off when the buzzer rang for the front door. It was Paul.

"Come on up," she said to him. Paul arrived a few seconds later with a beautiful bunch of pink roses. Josie answered the door still wrapped in her bath towel.

"Sorry I'm running late," she said securing her towel more tightly across her chest.

"These are for you," he said kissing her on the cheek.

"Thanks Paul, they're lovely. I'm sorry I'm not ready. Chrissie bought champagne to celebrate my new job and I didn't realise the time. I won't be long. Let me just put these in water first."

Paul followed her into the kitchen where she retrieved a vase from under the sink. As she began putting the roses into the vase, her towel, started to slip off. "Oops, sorry" she said covering her left breast which had become exposed.

"Don't apologise, you look lovely," he replied putting his arms on her shoulders and turning her towards him. He bent to kiss her and with that the whole towel fell off. Josie scrabbled to retrieve it but Paul held her shoulders tightly and just kept on kissing her. She couldn't resist his kisses and ignoring her complete nakedness, kissed him passionately back. His hands released her shoulders and moved down to caress her breasts. A groan escaped her lips as he circled her erect nipples delicately with his fingertips. Pulling back her wet hair and burying his mouth in her neck, he whispered, "You really are gorgeous Josie."

She was turned on by his kisses and caresses, but had no intention of having sex with Paul this early in their relationship. She moved away from him, pulling her towel back around her naked body.

She could see the confusion clouding his eyes.

"I'm sorry Paul. It's just too soon for me."

"No, of course, I'm the one who's sorry. I really didn't mean for that to happen, Josie," he said tenderly. "But you looked so beautiful with your towel slipping down, I just couldn't resist you."

She smiled, not knowing what else to say. 15 minutes later Josie emerged from her bedroom. Paul was sitting on the sofa, glancing through a women's magazine.

"Perhaps if I read more of these, I 'd have more success with women," he said, half jokingly.

"All any man need do is watch every episode of Sex in the City," she replied, trying to keep the conversation light. "Then you'll know everything you need to know. But it's a lot to take in, especially for the male brain. What with it being so small and all."

"Me Tarzan you Jane!" grunted Paul hooting like a caveman.

Josie couldn't help but laugh.

Outside in front of Paul's impressive vintage two-seater MGB CT V8, he asked her what she wanted to do. By now it was late evening and Josie realised she was starving. She had however sobered up from the wine and champagne she had drunk earlier.

"Let's go and get something to eat," she said, "my treat as you paid last time."

Paul suggested a popular restaurant called Chez Ma Cousine which was down one of the side streets in Montmarte.

"Leave your car here," she said, "we'll get there quicker by Métro."

Paul agreed and they walked hand in hand to the underground. As they emerged in Pigalle the streets were fairly quiet with few tourists. They walked up one of the side streets off the main thoroughfare to the steps at the bottom of the Sacré Coeur. Josie loved the beautiful white church with its stunning views of the city. Even on a drab, winter evening, the building glowed with a life of its own.

They walked up the steps, Paul pulling Josie as she flagged behind. "I need to exercise more," she said to herself as she huffed and puffed her way up. They headed for the Place du Têtre and then down another side street to the restaurant. They had no trouble getting a table and they shared a huge bowl of Moules Marinières for a starter, followed by steak and salad. Paul ordered a good bottle of red wine and Josie balked a bit at the price as the meal was supposed to be on her and she didn't usually pay that much for a bottle of wine. There was usually no need in Paris where the house wines were always excellent. Paul obviously wanted to show off his knowledge of good wines.

He insisted on paying for the meal anyway and became quite uppity when Josie tried to pay her share. "It's a man's place to pay," he told her firmly. She was surprised and chauvinism was not a trait she admired in men. She bit her tongue and let him pay but was quiet on the walk back down to the Métro.

"Is everything alright," Paul asked her, breaking the silence.

"Fine, I guess I'm just exhausted after a very exciting day," she replied, linking her arm in his, and realising she was being oversensitive about the paying thing.

Paul smiled down at her and kissed the top of her head. "Good, I thought I'd upset you for a moment there."

She told him that he hadn't and squeezed his arm for reassurance.

Back at the apartment, Josie invited Paul in for a coffee. Chrissie was still up watching a film and the three of them sat around for a while chatting and drinking coffee. Then Chrissie headed for bed.

Paul kissed her gently on the lips.

"I'd like to apologise again for earlier Josie. I really didn't mean to compromise you. I really like you and I don't want to rush you into anything, particularly with the Max thing still so fresh for you."

"Look Paul," she replied. "This has nothing to do with Max. I'm just not going to jump into bed with you at the drop of a hat. I need to get to know you first."

She knew she was being hypocritical as she had slept with Max after only knowing him a few hours. She hoped that Paul didn't know that as she didn't want him to think badly of her.

"I understand," he said, getting up from the sofa and reaching for his car keys.

Josie wasn't so sure that he did.

He kissed her on the cheek as she let him out of the front door.

"I'll call you tomorrow," he told her, "sleep tight."

"You too."

As she snuggled down in her bed, Josie had mixed feelings about Paul. She really enjoyed his company but had no intention of rushing into a full blown relationship with him, at least not yet. She just wasn't ready.

As she drifted off to sleep, she realised that Paul hadn't said anything to her about the rugby club do on Saturday. She knew all his mates would be going so he was likely to have bought a ticket. She resolved to ask him about it the next day.

Paul phoned her at the office lunchtime apologising for not calling earlier due to pressures at work. Josie asked him about the rugby club dance and Paul told her he was going back to the UK on Friday for a family wedding.

"I would ask you to go with me," he said to her, "but numbers are tight apparently. Sorry Josie, I would much rather spend the weekend with you."

"That's OK," she replied, "no problem." It was definitely too soon to be going with him to a family wedding and she was relieved that she didn't have to turn him down. "I was planning on going with Chrissie and Daniel anyway."

"Max will be there Josie so I'd rather you didn't go." Paul said firmly.

Josie was taken aback. They were hardly a couple yet and already he was telling her what to do. The chauvinistic moment in the restaurant came flooding back.

"Sorry Paul, but I made these arrangements before you and I had been out together. Also, I don't appreciate your trying to tell me what to do and if you don't trust me enough to go to a dance and keep my hands off Max then you can forget the whole thing." She hung up, angrier than she had felt in a long time.

"What's up?" Libby asked her. "Love's young dream not all it's cracked up to be?"

Josie told her what Paul had said and her friend was surprised. "Paul didn't strike me as the controlling sort," she said. "He seemed more switched on than that."

Josie was quite upset by the incident and headed for the loo to get her head straight. While she was in there, Libby shouted, "Paul's on the office phone for you."

"Tell him I'm in a meeting," she replied, "all afternoon."

Libby did that and Paul implored her to tell Josie he had called. By the time she got back to her desk there was a missed call, voicemail message and text message from him apologising for his crassness and offering to explain.

Josie waited a couple of hours and sent him a text asking him to call her at home that evening. He deserved the chance to explain and she would have calmed down by then. She still felt a bit disturbed at his attitude and, like Libby, hadn't picked up on this side of Paul before.

When they spoke later, he apologised profusely, explaining that he was just oversensitive where Max was concerned and that of course he trusted her. Josie guessed he wanted to say more about his feelings for her but didn't want to scare her off. To make up for it, he offered to cook a meal on Thursday evening which she agreed to.

"Paul, I'm sorry if I overreacted," she said, "I just hate to be told what I can or can't do. My parents can vouch for that."

Paul reassured her that she didn't need to apologise and gave her directions to his place from the Métro.

On Thursday evening she arrived on time with a reasonably decent bottle of wine.

Paul's apartment wasn't as luxurious as Max's but was in a better area. It was very clean and tidy and the smell of cooking coming from the small kitchen was delicious.

He hugged her as soon as she arrived and gave her a quick tour of the flat before leading her back into the living room and taking her in his arms again. They kissed for a while and Paul pulled away saying, "I'd better put you down now or dinner is going to be ruined."

Josie sat down and Paul brought her a gin and tonic. He joined her for a moment on the sofa, explaining that they were having couscous and hoped she liked it as he hadn't checked with her first. She told him that she loved it and he seemed delighted.

The food was glorious, he was obviously a very good cook and Josie told him so.

"It's what I wanted to do when I'd given up on the idea of becoming a pilot," he said. "But my dad said it wasn't a good job for a man and made me study accountancy. I hated it at University but enjoy my job now, so I guess he was right. I'm not sure I would have enjoyed the erratic social life of a busy chef, to be honest."

They cleared the table, stacked the dishes in the sink and Paul made a pot of coffee. He insisted he needed no help with the dishes which could wait and they returned to the sofa in the living room. Paul put on some music and pulled Josie to her feet. They danced slowly together, barely moving, just swaying in each others' arms.

When the music stopped, Paul kissed her passionately again. She returned his kisses with equal passion, but part of her remained detached. She just couldn't help it. Although she no longer wanted Max, she wasn't sure she wanted Paul either.

Eventually she pulled away from him, saying that she should make a move as it was getting very late. She could see the disappointment in his face and looked away embarrassed.

Paul wouldn't let her go home on the Métro and insisted on

calling a taxi. Josie really didn't want to have to pay for a taxi fare but refused point blank to allow him to pay, despite his insistence.

On the short journey home, she tried to make sense of her feelings for Paul. On the one hand, she did find him attractive, intelligent and socially very suitable but she knew in her heart of hearts that he wasn't the one for her, at least not at the moment. She was relieved that he would be going home at the weekend. It would give her some breathing space.

Paul called the next morning before leaving for the airport and told her to have a great weekend. He said he'd call again on Sunday to check how the party went and would see her next week. In return, she told him to have a good time himself.

Josie was very busy at work as Libby wasn't in. She phoned her friend just before lunch time to wish her the best of luck with Matt. Libby's excitement at seeing her lover was palpable and Josie was happy for her. She skipped lunch, working right through but decided to leave at 5pm on the dot despite there still being an awful lot of work still to get through.

Back at the flat, Chrissie had arrived a few minutes earlier and was rifling through the mail. She handed Josie a formal looking white envelope. It was the letter from Renseignements formerly offering her the job. The terms and conditions were as outlined by Thomas Frolin and Jacques Fredet and there were some additional perks like a health care plan and subsidized membership to a gym and tennis club.

They spent a quiet evening in and the next morning headed for the big department stores on Boulevard Haussman to find something to wear that night.

Chrissie didn't buy anything new but in true style, Josie found a red, off the shoulder top which would look great with her hip hugging black trousers.

The girls had an early supper and began to get ready for the do. Daniel was due at 8.30 pm and they were ready and waiting for him when he arrived. They had a quick drink in the apartment and headed for the rugby club hall which was on a side street off the bottom of the Champs Elysées. He dropped them off at the door as it was raining heavily by the time they arrived. The girls waited for him before going into the main bar. Josie couldn't help but feel nervous at the prospect of seeing Max again.

They each linked arms with Daniel and entered the main hall

which was packed. People were already dancing and the bar was at least five people deep. It reminded Josie of her days at University in the Students' Union bar. She had been expecting something a bit less 'rugbyish'- a bit more sophisticated.

Daniel found them a small table in the corner of the room and headed for the bar. He returned quickly as one of his mates had been at the front and had ordered the drinks for him. "Everyone sort of pitches up at once," he said to the girls apologetically "it's a bit of a scrum. But the bar will clear shortly and things will calm down. Cheers."

The girls raised their glasses, scanning the room. There were a lot of men there which cheered Josie up no end. "Lots of dance partners," she said to herself. Once they finished their drinks they danced with Daniel who after a few minutes returned to the bar which indeed had quietened down. Immediately two very drunk but very funny English guys started to dance with them and the girls had a really good time, fending off their half-hearted advances and just dancing and laughing.

When they eventually returned to their table Daniel was there chatting to a couple of men the girls didn't know. He introduced them as friends from the UK who came over regularly for the rugby matches with their respective, local clubs. The men, David and Patrick, joined the table and kept the girls entertained with tales of previous rugby trips to Paris and the escapades they had got into. They danced with the girls too and the evening sped by with rounds of drinks, dancing and general good humour. It was nearly midnight before Josie realised the time and that she hadn't clocked Max all evening. She scanned the room but couldn't see him, so turned her attentions back to Daniel, David and Patrick.

The drink was taking its toll and she headed for the loos which were off the main hall and down a long, winding corridor. She spent a few minutes in the loo splashing her face with cold water and then touching up her make up. She felt woozy and realised she was quite drunk but not slaughtered, well not yet anyway. She chuckled to herself.

As she emerged from the ladies, Max was standing outside as if he had been waiting for her. "You took your time," he said harshly blocking her way back down the narrow corridor.

"Make a habit of stalking women outside the ladies do you," she replied as steadily as she could. Her head was spinning and she was in no fit state for a confrontation with Max.

"You're nothing more than a common tart, Josie," he told her pushing his face close to hers. Even with the amount she had had to drink, she could tell he was in an even worse state than she was. "I saw you making up to those men like you couldn't wait to get their cocks inside you. Like a bitch on heat you……"

Josie slapped him hard across the cheek. He raised his hand to his face in disbelief and then raised his arm as if to hit her back. "Do that and you'll regret it," she said, standing her ground. In reality, she was terrified but she knew she couldn't let Max see that. Her words had the desired effect and he dropped his arm as if defeated.

"Oh God Josie, I'm sorry. I just can't bear to see you with other men. It's messing with my head. Please meet me again, just once at my place. For old times' sake."

"Not in a million years, Max. Now fuck off before I call Anna and tell her about 'us'. Trust me Max, I will," she said firmly. "I have nothing to lose and you have everything to lose. Just leave me alone."

"But I love you Josie," he cried out after her as she pushed her way past him and headed quickly down the corridor towards the main hall.

These were the words Josie had prayed he would say to her over the past few months. She didn't stop and look back, she daren't. She just carried on towards the main hallway. Josie made her way back to the table where David and Patrick were still regaling Chrissie and Daniel with hilarious stories. They were so drunk now they could barely string a sentence together which made it even funnier. Josie sat down with the others and tried to join in with the banter but her evening had been ruined. The party finished a little after 1am and Josie was relieved to be in a taxi with Chrissie and Daniel on their way home. Dan had decided to leave the car there and was going to kip down on the sofa at the girls' flat rather than go all the way back to his place.

Neither Chrissie nor Daniel noticed how quiet Josie was as they were pretty merry themselves and so she was able to slip off to bed without joining them for a nightcap. Despite the amount of alcohol she had consumed, she just couldn't sleep. The episode with Max had been disturbing and she felt wretched. Eventually she did drift off but woke early with a major hangover.

She got up, had some juice, pain killers and made a cup of tea.

Daniel was comatose on the sofa and there was no sound from Chrissie's room. She headed back to bed and checked her mobile. There was one text message, from Max, sent at 2 am that morning. Max apologised for his behaviour but confirmed that he meant what he said last night, that he did love her and would appreciate the opportunity to talk to her when they were both sober. On neutral ground if she preferred.

Josie didn't know what to do. She buried her head under the pillow, willing the thoughts flooding through her mind to go away. Then her mobile started ringing. It was Paul. She was tempted not to answer but she had to speak to him at some point. "Hi Paul," she replied trying to sound as cheery as possible, "you're up early for a Sunday."

"Hi babe I just wanted to check how last night went."

"Pretty good," she replied, "we met some of Daniel's friends who were really entertaining. The place was packed to the rafters, just like a student disco."

"And Max," Paul asked her. As no-one had seen them together she felt she could get away with saying that she hadn't seen him.

"I'm not sure he was even there," she told Paul, "it was so busy, if he was I didn't see him. How was the wedding?" she added quickly, changing the subject.

"Good, about Max I mean. The wedding was OK. My mum was desperately trying to get me fixed up with one of those Surrey horsy types who have loads of money but constantly stink of stables. I told her I had a serious girlfriend in Paris but that never stops her. I'll have to introduce you to her. She'll love you Josie and that will put a stop to her matchmaking. She's dying for grandchildren and I'm her main hope on that front."

This was all too much for Josie. "Serious girlfriend and meeting his mum, children…" she said to herself. We've only known each other 10 seconds. All this on top of Max telling her he loved her. She just couldn't cope and groaned out load.

"What's wrong Josie, are you OK?"

"I have a bit of a headache," she replied, which was not untrue. "I didn't sleep very well and I'm still in bed Paul. I'm going to try to get some shut eye. Shall I call you later?"

She could sense his disapproval. "As long as you didn't misbehave," he almost scolded her. Josie wanted to laugh out loud, she felt like a naughty schoolgirl. "Call me this evening before dinner," he ordered, "say around seven. OK?"

"Sure, speak to you later, bye." And she hung up before he could say any more.

The phone rang again immediately and she answered it without looking at the screen. "I'll call you at seven Paul, I promise" she said, "now please leave me to get some sleep."

"It's Max, not Paul. Please don't hang up Josie, I desperately want to speak to you. Look I'm really, really sorry about last night. I was totally out of order and very drunk, or I wouldn't have behaved so abysmally. But I did mean it when I said 'I love you'. Please meet me so I can talk to you. It doesn't have to be my place. I'll meet you anywhere, you say where and when."

She looked at her watch. It was only 9 am. "OK," she replied, "11 am in the Café Sancerre."

"I'll be there waiting for you," he replied and hung up.

She lay there in her bed for a few minutes thinking about both Max and Paul. She knew it was betraying Paul to meet Max but the former was moving too fast for her and his possessiveness made her feel quite uncomfortable.

Eventually she got out of bed and had a shower. Daniel and Chrissie were still asleep when she left the apartment. She arrived at the café 10 minutes early but Max was already there, looking very nervous, she noted.

He stood up to greet her, giving her a peck on the cheek. Her skin literally burned at his touch and she was amazed at how he could still make her feel this way despite everything he had said and done.

He ordered them both a coffee and launched straight away into what seemed like a rehearsed speech. He told her that he and Anna had split up after the surprise party for a number of reasons. Anna had told him she expected to get engaged at the party and this had made him realise he didn't love her and didn't want to spend the rest of his life with her. She had moved her belongings out of his flat and he hadn't heard from her since.

"I just can't get you out of my mind Josie," he said. "Seeing you with Paul made me so jealous, it was unbearable. I'll be honest. I don't know how things will work out and I know I have a lot of bridges to build with you, but I really want to try and make a go of it. Be like a normal couple. What do you say?"

Josie was shocked. She really wasn't expecting this. As strong as her feelings for Max had been, she still didn't trust him entirely. Also, for his sake, it was too soon after ending the relationship with Anna to just head straight into another.

Taking a deep breath, she told him how she felt, "Max, I think it would be a mistake to rush straight back into a relationship. I think you should take a bit of time to yourself and be certain about what you really want. I will be totally honest with you, Paul is moving too fast for me and it's not fair to lead him on when I don't know what I want. So when he gets back, I am going to tell him that and cool things right down."

Max reached across the table and gently took her hand.

"I'm not sure myself what I want, I'm very confused. I thought I wanted you but now I'm not sure," he tried to interrupt but she silenced him by putting her finger to his mouth. "Let me finish."

"I'll meet you for an occasional coffee and chat on the phone if you wish, but I'm not hopping straight back into bed with you. As for Paul, I will tell him truthfully that we need to take a break."

Max nodded and smiled.

Then something occurred to her. "Max, does Paul know that you and Anna have split up?"

"I guess so," Max replied, "all the gang must know by now."

That would explain Paul not wanting her to go to the dance Josie reasoned. He was afraid Max would persuade her to get back with him.

"If that's what you want Josie, I understand."

Josie raised a sceptical eyebrow.

"No, I truly do," said Max, laughing. "I don't expect you to jump straight back into bed with me but hopefully one day you will," he added with the old Max charm.

Josie couldn't help but smile at him. "We'll see. I'll call you after I've spoken to Paul tomorrow and then maybe we can meet for a coffee again next Sunday?"

"Next Sunday, but that's ages away. Can't we meet earlier?" he pleaded.

"Don't push it Max, or I won't meet you at all."

"OK, have it your way," he sounded like a sulky school boy.

Josie stood up to leave and Max reached over to kiss her cheek again. She turned her face towards him and his lips brushed hers. It was like a lightning bolt going through her. "Oh God," she said to herself quickly leaving the café without looking back, "I just hope I can resist him until I know what I really want."

To clear her head, Josie decided to walk back to the apartment. She had been walking for a good half an hour when Chrissie phoned, checking where she was.

"I'll be home soon," she told her friend.

When she arrived back at the flat, Chrissie was preparing a cooked breakfast brunch.

"Where have you been?" Chrissie asked her.

"Just out and about," she replied. She felt completely drained and couldn't face long explanations.

They ate their breakfast and then Josie said she hadn't slept very well so was going for a kip. She slept all afternoon and woke around 5 pm.

Josie stumbled groggily into the sitting room, Chrissie was snuggled up on the sofa in a warm blanket watching a popular French TV quiz 'Des Chiffres et Des Lettres', equally well known in the UK as 'Count Down'.

Chrissie looked at her flat mate, expecting an explanation. Josie sighed. Grabbed half of the blanket and settling herself onto the other half of the sofa, resigned to tell Chrissie everything.

"I can't believe it," exclaimed Chrissie. "Talk about using people... well women. Who the hell does he think he his?"

"I know," replied Josie, "that's why I'm keeping him at arm's-length for the moment. A few weeks ago I would have died and gone to Heaven to hear Max tell me that he loves me. But too much has happened since. It's only a week or so since he and Anna have split up, they may still get back together."

"And Paul?" asked Chrissie sharply.

"I do like Paul and it would be easy to slip into a relationship with him but I have some reservations, like his moving too fast and his possessiveness. So when he's back I'm going to tell him that I need some time. Whether he will associate it with Max or not, I don't know."

"Poor you," said Chrissie putting her arm around Josie's shoulders, "life is never straightforward for you is it?"

Josie shook her head.

At seven o'clock prompt, Josie phoned Paul. "See," she told her flat mate, "I'm completely conforming to his orders and anxious that he'll be cross if I don't call at the right time!"

Chrissie rolled her eyes and stifled a laugh.

Paul seemed delighted to hear from her and Josie felt awful knowing she was going to cool down the relationship when she next saw him.

"You're very quiet, Josie," he said, "I normally I can't get a word in edgeways."

"Just tired I guess," she replied, "too many late nights. What time are you back tomorrow?"

"I should be back home by 4 pm at the latest. Do you fancy popping round after work?"

"OK," she thought it was probably best to get the conversation over and done with as soon as possible for both their sakes.

CHAPTER 11

The next day at work was busy and as Libby was still off, Josie had no time to ponder over what she was going to say to Paul. She did however manage to get her letter of resignation typed up, giving one month's notice. This would enable her to start at Renseignements on 1st March.

JC accepted the letter and told her that he knew she would be happy there. "You will need to get a cart de séjour as you won't be paid from the UK any longer. You knows that, right?"

Josie nodded, just another thing to add her list of things to do before she started at Renseignements – the main task being to sort out her love life.

She finished later than she would have liked and sent a text to Paul just as she was leaving.

Josie arrived at his apartment at 6 pm and Paul was delighted to see her, wrapping her up in his arms and giving her a huge hug. "I did miss you Josie," he told her, holding her at arm's length and smiling into her eyes. "Did you miss me?"

Josie looked away, feeling like a real shit, unable to hold his gaze. Paul sensed immediately that something was wrong.

"What's up babe? I can tell something's wrong. Come on talk to me," he said pulling her down next to him on the sofa.

"I'm really sorry Paul, but this…you and I …. It's just moving too fast for me. I do really like you but I'm not ready for a serious relationship at the moment and it seems unfair to lead you on when I'm not sure what I want."

The expression on Paul's face turned quickly from astonishment to anger.

"I suppose this is all about Max is it Josie?"

"No it isn't Paul. It has nothing to do with Max. It's to do with me and you and that's it. I have to say you scared me off with your comments about meeting your mum and all that."

She did feel guilty lying to him as in her heart of hearts she knew it was partly due to Max.

Paul's face was like stone. "Max was right, Josie. You are a prick tease. You led me to believe you felt something for me. You can't treat people like that. It's wrong."

Josie felt even more guilty. Paul's words were hurtful but she had to admit to herself that there was an element of truth in them.

"I'm sorry you feel that way Paul," she said standing up and reaching for her handbag. "I really didn't mean to hurt you or lead you on. I thought we were just having a bit of fun, nothing too serious."

"Is that it then?" he spat.

"Well, it's up to you. If you want to see me again, that's fine but it will be as friends, at least for the moment. Look, I'll give you a call later in the week and perhaps we can meet for lunch."

Paul didn't reply. He just turned away from her stare out the window, lost in his own thoughts.

"Bye Paul," she said to his back and let herself out of the apartment. As she headed for the Métro, she called the flat to tell Chrissie she was on her way home. Back home she told her all about Paul and his reaction.

Later that evening Libby phoned and sounded really depressed. Josie asked why and she said she'd explain the next day. "We both have a lot of catching up to do tomorrow then Libby," Josie said to her friend. "It's amazing what can happen in just a few days."

As JC wasn't in the next morning, the girls spent the best part of their time catching up on the weekend's events. Libby was amazed at Max and Anna splitting up but wasn't surprised that Josie had ditched Paul.

"I guessed from your reaction the other evening that he was too possessive for you," she said to Josie, "He would have stifled you in the end. Complete control freak or what?"

"I guess you're right. So Libby, tell me all about your weekend with Matt, was it wonderful?"

Libby filled Josie in on the details of the weekend with Matt which seemed to have been spent mainly in bed. Libby hadn't wanted to rock the boat by asking Matt how he had managed to get away but hated the times when he 'sneaked off' to phone home. As much as she loved him, she did feel awful betraying his and her families in this way and wasn't sure if she could continue with the affaire, particularly as she was about to return to the UK where the chances of meeting would increase considerably.

"I asked him yesterday morning if there would ever be any future for us," Libby told her friend. "He just looked at me with such sad eyes and told me that if circumstances were different, then yes but he simply couldn't leave Lia and the boys. It would be the scandal of the village."

Josie was sympathetic and did understand what Libby was going through.

"I told him that I didn't think I could continue having an affaire with him but he said that even if we only have snatched moments, then surely that was better than nothing. I just didn't know what to say. I can't imagine life without him but I hate hiding our love away like this. I just don't know what to do."

Josie thought it wasn't dissimilar to how she felt about Max. She was confused about him and decided that the best course of action was to steer clear for a while to avoid any upsets. She was concerned that Paul would find out that she knew about Max and Anna's break up and wished she hadn't lied to him but it was too late now.

The rest of the week was pretty uneventful. Josie couldn't bring herself to call Paul to arrange lunch so she took the cowardly option and sent him a text saying that she was thinking of him and if he wanted to meet up to give her a call. He didn't call and Josie wasn't sure if she was glad or sad.

Chrissie had arranged for Claude and his best friend Christian to come for supper on Saturday evening which gave Josie something to look forward to. "No trying to fix me up," she told her friend, "I've had enough of men for the time being."

"That will be the day," said Chrissie rolling her eyes.

It was Saturday afternoon before she realised that Max hadn't been in touch all week and that they had tentatively arranged to meet on the Sunday for coffee. "Maybe he's back with Anna," thought Josie.

She didn't know why by his lack of attention bugged her and niggled at the back of her mind all day. Several times she started to send him a text but stopped herself as it would seem like she was chasing him.

The supper went well and the company was really great. They all got very drunk and they had an impromptu disco in the sitting room using the fairy lights from the Christmas tree as strobe-type lighting.

At one point, Chrissie couldn't find her watch and thought it had come off her wrist while shaking the table cloth out of the window. The boys started leaning out of the sitting room window which overlooked a small courtyard, only accessible from the ground floor flat and throwing lighted matches down to see if they could see the watch. Claude then tried drunkenly to get out of the window to climb down the drainpipe to find the watch. Fortunately Chrissie was able to stop him before he did himself any damage. The whole episode was ridiculously silly but everyone found it completely hysterical. They only stopped their antics when their neighbour below started screaming at them to be quiet, which made them all laugh even more.

It was gone 2 am before they realised the time and so Christian crashed in the sitting room while the others all went to bed. Christian gave Josie a soppy, drunken kiss as she headed unsteadily from the bathroom to her bedroom.

"I would love to wake up next to you in the morning, beautiful English girl," he said.

Josie wasn't so drunk that she was going to fall for that one. "In your dreams, handsome French man. You'll have to wake up on the sofa, thank you very much."

Christian laughed and gave her another sloppy kiss before falling back onto the sofa as if his legs could no longer hold him.

The next morning Josie was woken up by the sound of her mobile beeping in her handbag. She looked at her watch, it was 9 am. Her head was pounding as she struggled to get up. The text message was from Max confirming their meeting at 11 am.

Josie had assumed it was off as she hadn't heard from him all week. Last night the girls had arranged with the boys to go out to Fontainbleau where they could hire bikes and cycle through the forest. She had missed the last jaunt with the air traffic controllers because she was meeting Max, she didn't intend to miss this one.

Josie sent a text back saying that she had made other plans as she hadn't heard from him. Within minutes Max was ringing her.

"But you said not to contact you, Josie," he said, "so I respected your wishes. As I hadn't heard from you I thought I'd better confirm the arrangements and now you say you can't make it. Surely you can cancel your other plans? I really want to see you."

"Sorry Max, but no, I'm not letting my friends down."

"Oh so it's OK to let me down but not your friends. That's great, thanks a bunch."

Josie did feel a bit guilty and wished that she had sent a text to Max the day before. "Look, I'll make it up to you. How about we meet tomorrow evening after work for a drink?"

"Why not tonight?" Max shot back firmly.

Josie didn't know what time they would be back from Fontainbleau and didn't want to be clock watching all afternoon. She told Max this and he started pressing her about where she was going and with whom.

Josie was starting to get angry.

"Look Max, I'm not accountable to you in anyway. Where I go and with whom is my business. I'm happy to meet you tomorrow evening but if you don't want to then fine. No problem."

He backed down then and agreed to meet her the following evening in Harry's Bar off the Place de l'Opéra. "Perhaps we can have dinner too?" he asked tentatively.

"We'll see," she replied, "see you tomorrow at six."

When she came off the phone, Josie didn't know whether to be pleased or cross with Max. He obviously really wanted to see her and had respected her wish to be left alone. But she wasn't going to let him take over her life, not by any means. She lay in bed dozing for the next couple of hours, eventually getting up when she heard voices from the sitting room.

Chrissie was up and had made some coffee. Everyone looked and felt really rough. The boys decided to go home to shower and change before meeting at Fontainbleau. They arranged to meet Josie and Chrissie at the cycle hire place at 2 pm. Josie phoned Libby and invited her along too. She was pleased as she had declined the invitation for supper the previous evening due to a longstanding arrangement with Madame Vergne to attend the ballet. Libby admitted that it had been pretty tame compared with the evening the others had shared.

After showers and lunch, the girls set off for the Métro and arrived at Fontainbleau with plenty of time. They all hired bikes and the cycle through the woods was invigorating but tiring. Josie realised how unfit she was and vowed to make maximum use of the subsidised gym facilities when she started at Renseignements. She was really looking forward to starting her new job. Life felt good and if only she could sort out her love life, then it would be even better.

"I think I'll avoid men for the moment," she thought to herself as they continued to cycle through the forest. They stopped for a rest next to a pretty river running through the woods. Josie sat down, leaning against a tree and closed her eyes. Christian came and sat next to her.

"Would you like to come out for dinner with me one night this week?" he asked her. "I really like you Josie and I think we could have some fun together."

"I'd love to," she replied immediately, all her resolve going out of the window. She did enjoy Christian's company. He was funny and lively and very good looking, in a dark Southern French sort of way. He didn't seem like he would be too serious like Paul and she knew from Claude that he was single.

"How about Friday then, I'm not working the next day?"

"Friday's good," she replied, "where shall we go?"

"I'll call you," he told her and brushed her cheek gently with his lips. She didn't feel the same frisson that she had felt when Max had kissed her the week before but the kiss was sweet and gentle.

"You'll have to give me some idea so I know what to wear," she told him teasingly.

"Les femmes!" he said throwing his arms up in exasperation. "You women always so concerned about your appearance. Don't worry it will be nothing too formal and we won't be walking through forests and fields either, so somewhere in between."

"OK," Josie replied coyly as Christian touched her face gently and smiled. After a few minutes, they all set off on their bikes again. Libby cycling alongside Josie commented on how cosy she and Christian seemed together.

"I'm going out to dinner with him on Friday evening," she

told her friend.

"Great, that should help take your mind off Max and Paul. I wish I could find someone to help take my mind off Matt."

Josie didn't have the heart to tell Libby that she gave out a certain aura of 'don't come near me' to most men. The second anyone tried to chat her up, her defences went up and most men were put off from the word go. Chrissie sometimes performed a hilarious send up of Libby being 'overly prickly' as she described it. This normally had Josie in fits of giggles and even Libby had to admit there was some truth in it.

"You need to go more with the flow, Libby," Josie told her carefully. "I mean you were quite off with this lot the first night we met them and they're all pretty good guys and great fun. You're enjoying yourself in their company aren't you?"

"You're right, I know. I just find it hard to trust people… well men especially. I don't know why. It's not as though a man has ever treated me really badly. It was different with Matt of course as I knew him already. I don't know it's just me I guess. I wish I could be more like you."

"What completely confused and torn between two, no three men. I wouldn't wish that on anyone!"

Libby laughed and the friends sped up on their bikes to catch the others up. A few hours later, when they had given the bikes back, they headed for a local café for a well-earned drink. By this time it was nearly 6 pm and the guys, who were working the early shift the next day, said they should go home.

They all walked to the underground together and then split up to take different trains home. Libby came back to the flat with the girls and they mustered up a quick omelette for supper. While they were eating the telephone just didn't stop ringing. First it was Daniel saying he'd been trying to get hold of them all day. Then it was Josie's parents calling for an update from their daughter. Claude called Chrissie who was on the phone for ages, giggling and laughing. While they were clearing up, the phone rang again. It was Paul for Josie.

She really didn't feel like talking to him but Chrissie had said she was in and so she couldn't avoid it.

"Hi Paul," she said trying to sound cheery.

"Hi Josie I just wanted to call to say sorry for not getting in touch last week but I was really upset after our conversation on

Monday. I wondered if we could meet tomorrow after work for a drink. I really want to talk to you."

"Oh no," she thought, "bloody typical. I'm seeing Max tomorrow evening. What the hell shall I say?"

"Are you still there Josie," Paul asked worried by her silence.

"Sorry Paul, I can't tomorrow how about another evening?"

"I'm away the rest of the week at a conference." He said expectantly.

Josie felt really bad. She didn't want to keep lying to Paul but she couldn't tell him she was meeting Max as this would hurt him even more.

"Sorry I can't Paul, it's to do with my new job and I can't get out of it."

"Well how about Friday evening then?"

Josie groaned inwardly, how had she managed to get herself into such a mess. Thinking quickly she replied, "Sorry Paul but the girls and I have tickets for the ballet, it's been planned ages ago. How about Saturday?"

"It's the cricket club dinner on Saturday. I had assumed you would be going with me but of course things have changed now, haven't they?" he said coldly.

As much as she hated the thought of spending another evening at the cricket club, Josie felt she owed it to Paul to go with him.

"I can still come with you if you want me to," she told him, hoping that wouldn't be the case.

"Are you sure? Max will probably be there."

"So, what difference does that make," she said, knowing that it did. She would have to tell Max that she was going to the dinner with Paul. She wondered whom Max would be going with.

"Well, he'll probably be with his new woman anyway." Paul said as if reading her thoughts.

"New woman?" Josie was stunned. "What new woman?"

"Haven't you heard? I thought Daniel would have filled you in on all the gory details. Anna and Max have split up. She caught him with another woman in his flat, a Spanish girl by all accounts. Apparently she had suspected for a while that he had been playing around," he said sarcastically, "and then caught him red handed. Or bare arsed if you like. I gather Max has tried to get her back but Anna's not stupid and realised what a shit he really was. Sorry,

Josie, I thought you knew." He finally said, sounding quite the opposite of sorry.

In her state of shock, Josie was speechless.

"I imagine it doesn't come as any great surprise to you Josie," Paul said, "I mean knowing Max as intimately as you do."

Josie could detect a certain note of satisfaction in Paul's voice.

"So Max had been lying to her as well," she thought to herself, no longer listening to Paul. "Why was he so miffed the day before when she cancelled their date? And why had he given her a totally different version of events?"

"Josie, are you listening to me," the raised tone of Paul's voice made her start.

"Sorry Paul, what were you saying?"

"I was saying that you had a lucky escape there. It could have been you caught with Max and that would have been very embarrassing. You might have found yourself ostracized after all it's a rather small community of us Brits over here."

Josie didn't need reminding of the fact, least of all from Paul. "Look Paul, I've told you before. I know I made a mistake with Max and I've learned my lesson. There's no need to be nasty about it."

"I'm sorry," said Paul who did actually sound contrite. "To be honest it did cross my mind that you split with me because you knew that Max and Anna had broken up. But knowing you, Josie, I realised you wouldn't be that shallow or stupid. If he can do it to Anna, play away I mean. He can do it to anyone. She really stood by him when he was in the shit at work and I thought he would have treated her better than this."

Josie had never really got to the bottom of what had happened to make Max so indebted to Anna. "What did happen?" she asked Paul. "I've heard snippets but not the full story."

"He was accused of embezzling some funds from a big client. Now Max maybe a lot of things but a thief he isn't. Also this was a brilliant scam and Max doesn't have the brains to have thought something up like this. But all the evidence pointed to him. Anna knew Max from University, they weren't going out then, and she persuaded her boss from the law firm to take on Max's case and won it for him. He was suspended from work with no pay and nowhere to live, so Anna took him in. That's when the relationship started. Once he was cleared, he moved back into his flat.

Everyone thought he'd stay living at Anna's but I guess that would have cramped his style."

"He's a real bastard, isn't he?" Josie said, more to herself than to Paul.

"He can be. I think he's very insecure and needs the attention of lots of people to counteract that insecurity. He's the same with men and women, enough about Max. You will come with me on Saturday then?"

"Yes I will," said Josie decisively. A plan to get back at Max was forming in her mind and going to the dinner would be an essential part of that plan.

"I'll give you a ring Saturday morning to confirm the arrangements."

When she hung up, she sat in the hallway for a while thinking about what Paul had told her. She then went back into the sitting room and told the girls. Josie also told them what she had in mind to get back at Max for deceiving her. Her intention was to embarrass him in front of his new woman by claiming to be his girlfriend. She felt so utterly betrayed by him that she was prepared to make herself look stupid for the sheer pleasure of seeing him squirm.

"What an absolute shit. I'd love to be a fly on the wall at the dinner next week," Chrissie told her. "Just to see his face."

"I'm going to have to be careful how I play this in front of Paul though."

"Well yes, he is taking you after all," said Chrissie, "you don't want to show him up. It's Max you need to sock it to."

"Didn't Max realise that I would find out eventually. I guess he wanted to brainwash me first so I saw his side of the story."

"How do you feel about him now?" Libby asked.

"My initial reaction, after the shock, was anger but now I can see him for what he really is and I'm glad I didn't fall straight into his arms when he told me he loved me. I still don't know what he's playing at but I'll find out eventually."

The next day dragged by as Josie was both anxious and nervous about convincing Max that nothing was up, otherwise her plan wouldn't work.

She arrived first and ordered herself a Margheurita for some Dutch courage. Max arrived shortly after and ordered the same. He sat next to her on the bench and reached over to kiss her on the lips. It was all Josie could do not to wipe her mouth in disgust.

Max asked what she had been up to and when she was going to start her new job. She told him that she wasn't seeing Paul any more. Max naturally assumed it was because of him and became almost unbearable. She managed to bite her tongue and eventually she was able to steer the conversation around to the cricket club dinner.

"I know it may be awkward if Anna is there Max but I'm more than happy to go to the cricket club dinner with you on Saturday night. I'd hate to think of you there alone without a date." The look of horror on Max's face was a picture. "Thanks Josie but I didn't dare ask you as you said you wanted to take things slowly and you did say you didn't want me to get in touch."

Josie noticed with some satisfaction that Max was starting to sweat.

"I've asked one of the girls from work to go with me. A colleague you wouldn't know her - absolutely nothing in it of course. It would be very difficult to take back the invitation now. Sorry, I would much rather have gone with you."

"He's smooth," thought Josie, "really smooth."

"Such a shame," she feigned disappointment. "I thought this could be our first official date as a couple."

"A couple, but I thought…," he trailed off as if unsure of what he thought.

"Still I suppose it wouldn't be fair to Anna to flaunt me in her face would it. So probably best that I don't go with you anyway. You behave yourself Max I don't want this work colleague getting the wrong idea."

Max was looking a bit bewildered. Josie's plan was working. She guessed that he believed that because he was no longer with Anna she would happily slip back into bed with him with no strings attached. It went a long way to proving just how little he really thought of her.

Josie could tell that Max was feeling uncomfortable with her change of heart. She continued chatting about the fun they would have now they could be together. Max was starting to look really concerned.

"Max are you alright? You've turned white and your sweating buckets." Josie dabbed at his forehead with her napkin.

"It must be these Margheuritas," he said nervously, "they've gone straight to my head."

"Where are we going for dinner then?" she asked him, prepared to prolong the evening just to see him squirm even more.

"Oh sorry Josie, I didn't realise you were up for dinner. I thought it was just a drink. I've arranged a game of squash later with one of the boys."

"Likely story," she thought, "OK. Well I'm away for the rest of the week with work," she lied. Josie didn't want to spend any more time with him than she had to. "I'll call you lots," she said as she snuggled up to him.

"Right," he said awkwardly, "but I have a mega busy week so if my mobile is off just leave me a message."

"Sure, of course," Josie smiled. "But I can call you on your landline now the coast is all clear, can't I?"

Again, she enjoyed watching Max squirm. "Well yes, though I've been having some problems with my landline, the mobile's your best bet. You'll always get me then when I'm out and about. No point phoning the landline."

They finished their drinks and left the bar together, Josie clinging possessively to Max's arm.

"It's so good to have you all finally to myself," she said just to make him even more uncomfortable than he already was.

They parted company at the Métro with Josie promising to call him every day. When she arrived home, she told Chrissie that the plan seemed to be working and what a pleasure it had been to see Max obviously feeling very uncomfortable.

The rest of the week passed quickly with Josie calling Max every evening on his mobile. It was switched off most of the time but Josie left upbeat, chatty messages and most evenings Max called her back. Sometimes he was open and chatty and other times he was more reticent. Josie put this down to when his new woman was around. She was still confused about Max's behaviour towards her. He seemed so angry on the Saturday at the rugby club do and then when they met for coffee on the Sunday he had again seemed genuinely to care for her. She just didn't understand him at all. However, she was no longer 'bewitched' by him and suspected that although Max was not interested in her full time, he didn't want anyone else to have her either.

On Friday evening, she met Christian as arranged at the top of the Champs Elysées and they headed for a Pizzeria which was considered the best in Paris. It was a big, busy place and not the ideal location for a romantic dinner for two. Josie was glad. She did like Christian and he was a really good laugh, but she'd had enough of romance for the moment. Friendship and fun were the order of the day for the foreseeable future.

The evening passed by very quickly with Christian telling Josie tales about the air traffic controllers exploits. "It's enough to put me off flying forever," she told him, following a particularly funny incident in the control tower involving a practical joke on one of the controllers which had gone horribly wrong.

After their meal, they strolled down the busy Avenue, bustling with locals and tourists out on a Friday night. Christian suggested going to a night club but Josie declined. She had a busy day on the Saturday and then the dinner too. Christian offered to take her home but Josie turned him down again. It wasn't too late and she was happy to take the Métro on her own. Christian told her that he had really enjoyed her company and would like to take her out again soon. Josie said that it had been a perfect evening and she would love to go out with him again. He had been funny and clever but above all - not too pushy.

As they said their goodbyes, Christian leaned toward her and kissed her very gently on the mouth. "La belle Josephine," he said. "Beautiful Josie, until we meet again." He was acting so cheesy, it was funny. He pretended to be hurt when Josie laughed at him but the twinkle in his eyes told her he wasn't taking himself too seriously.

When she arrived home Chrissie had already gone to bed. As she prepared for bed herself, she thought about the evening with Christian and how relaxed it had been and what a lovely man he was. Good looking too. It took her ages to get off to sleep as she couldn't stop thinking about the cricket dinner the next night and her plan to humiliate Max.

The following day, after a much needed visit to the supermarket to stock up on essentials, the girls split up and Josie went to the hairdressers. None of these preparations made her feel better. She was getting more and more nervous as the day went on. She had spoken to Paul earlier and he had been quite 'off' with her, saying that he may cancel as he was so tired from work. Josie persuaded him that it would be a good evening and hoped there wouldn't be too much come back from him when he discovered why she really wanted to go to the party.

Originally, her plan was dependent on Paul being out of the way but she knew this would be difficult so had resigned herself to the fact that he would probably realise what she was up to. She just hoped he took it the right way, she didn't want to hurt him but her need for revenge on Max was overwhelming.

Paul picked her up promptly at 7.30 pm and complimented her on her appearance. Josie was wearing a classic black cocktail dress that showed off her legs and bust and made her waist look really small. She was wearing black and white pearl earrings and necklace and high, black court shoes. "A bit funereal," she had said to herself looking in the mirror before Paul arrived, "but very appropriate."

They arrived at the club by 8.00 pm and unlike last time, there was no-one hovering, on the lookout from the veranda. Josie followed Paul into the main room where tables were laid for dinner with table plans on boards in the doorway. Josie and Paul checked their table and she was relieved to see that Max was not seated with them. The table plan read, 'Max Williamson and partner'. Scanning the room, Josie couldn't see him but then only a handful of people had arrived so far, there was plenty of time. She had also noted that Anna's name was not on any of the table plans and wasn't surprised. "It must be horrible for her," thought Josie who had never thought about the other woman's feelings before then.

Josie found a spot in the room where she had full view of the door but couldn't be easily seen herself. She and Paul chatted for a while and then were joined by some other couples whom Paul knew. Josie only half participated in the conversation, keeping her eye on the door. Ten minutes later Max arrived with a stunning, dark haired girl on his arm. She was obviously Spanish and was extremely petite, with very long, glossy dark hair which she wore loose down her back.

Josie waited until Max had bought drinks and was chatting in a group before quietly making her way over to him. She tapped him on the shoulder and his face when he turned around was a picture. "Hi Max," she said, "surprise, surprise."

Max was speechless. He quickly glanced at the girl he had arrived with. She was engrossed in conversation with one of his friends.

"Josie what the hell are you doing here?" he said angrily.

"I came with Paul," she told him. "He was so disappointed when we split. I agreed last minute to come along tonight. Besides I thought it would give me the chance to spend some time with you Max. We haven't seen each other all week. What's wrong? I thought you'd be pleased."

She saw his Spanish friend, glance over at them questioningly. "Aren't you going to introduce me, Max," she asked, moving past him and smiling at the dark haired girl.

Before he could stop her, Josie was holding out her hand. "Hi, I'm Josie, Max's girlfriend."

The girl's expression went from surprise, to complete bewilderment. She looked at Max quizzically. "Not exactly, girlfriend, in that sense," he said to her hurriedly, "you know, a friend who is a girl."

"I dunna understand Massimilio," said the young woman in a thick Spanish accent. Max was looking increasingly uncomfortable, "Qui es? Who is this woman?"

"No-one," replied Max, looking from one woman to the other. Josie was enjoying this.

Max was blustering, caught out for the lying cheating rat that he was.

"Oh Max, you are funny, "Josie continued, clinging to his arm. "One minute you tell me you love me and the next you pretend we're not an item. That's men for you," she said directly to the girl who was now looking completely confused and staring questioningly at Max.

Around them, the group had stopped their own conversations and were listening intently to the mini-drama unfolding in front of them. Most of them knew why Max and Anna had split but the added element of Josie was making this a very entertaining episode in the saga. Paul had also joined the group and was looking as confused as the Spanish girl.

"Aren't you going to introduce me to your friend? I gather you're a work colleague of Max's?" Josie said directly to her.

"Max, what is going on here? I am very confused," her voice was very deep for such a small woman and her accent incredibly strong.

"I can explain, Lorenza,"

"Yes please do," said Josie, enjoying the look of horror on Max's face.

Turning to Josie he said, "Look Josie, I only took you out for a coffee and a drink because I felt sorry for you. You can't seem to hold down a relationship of any kind and you were always pestering me, even when I was with Anna. I just think you've got the wrong end of the stick. I was only trying to be kind."

"Bravo Max, you really ought to be on the stage," Josie replied. "I'm sure you'd win an Oscar. You're quite the thespian."

"Perhaps it's time you went home Josie," said Max. "I think you're really making an embarrassment of yourself."

"Really," Josie replied. "Well how do you explain this then."
Josie had her mobile phone in her hand and on loudspeaker played back the messages Max had left her over the past couple of weeks. Including the one telling her that he loved her.

Looking Max directly in the eye she said, "I feel sorry for you Max, I truly do. You really don't appreciate a good thing when you have it."

Turning to his new girlfriend, she apologised for embarrassing her and said, "He's not worth it, dear, trust me."

Josie headed for the bar in pursuit of a much needed drink and Paul was right behind her.

"What the hell was all that about? Was this a set up?"

Josie felt bad. She really didn't want to hurt Paul but needed to hurt Max more.

"Sorry Paul, I really did want to come to the dinner with you. Max has been pestering me for weeks to go out with him and I had agreed to have a drink with him on Monday night. He told me about the split with Anna but I didn't know the circumstances until you told me on Sunday evening. I did have a drink with him but he said nothing about being caught with this girl so I thought I'd get some revenge on him for being such a bastard, not just to me but to women in general."

Although this wasn't the whole truth, it was close enough for Paul to buy it. He was still upset though. "So you did use me Josie. You know what, you are no better than him."

"I really didn't mean to use you Paul. I had already agreed to go to the dinner with you before I knew Max was bringing someone else tonight. It just all fitted into place. Can't you understand my need for revenge? He has been hounding me for weeks. The bastard probably thought I'd just hop back into bed with him so he could continue to have the best of both worlds. He was so wrong."

"So ending us was nothing to do with Max and Anna splitting up then?"

Josie felt she had hurt him enough without admitting that it did have a small part to play in it at the time.

"Absolutely not Paul," she hoped he wouldn't realise that the messages she had just played from Max on her mobile were left the weekend before she ended their relationship. "As I said, I'm just not ready for anything too serious at the moment but, if you'd like to, we can keep seeing each other as friends. And who knows, I may realise the error of my ways!"

Paul smiled at her but his eyes remained sad. "Josie, we could be so good together. I guess I'll have to live with friends if that's what you want but I will always want more… you know that."

She smiled and reached up to kiss him on the cheek. Out of the corner of her eye she could see Max and Lorenza out on the veranda. They were in the middle of what looked like a humdinger of a row. She indicated to Paul to look too. At that moment, the Spanish girl slapped Max hard across his face and practically tore his shirt in two, buttons popping all over the veranda. Lorenza stormed out of the club. After a few moments, he followed her more slowly and the couple didn't reappear again that evening.

Although Josie's plan had worked, she didn't feel all that great. Revenge was not as sweet as she thought it would be and she had hurt Paul who didn't deserve to be treated so badly. She couldn't wait for the dinner to be over so they could leave. Paul too was very quiet which made Josie feel even worse than before.

After coffee, whilst some presentation speeches were going on, Josie headed for the ladies. She hadn't drunk much but was feeling completely drained. While she was touching up her make up a group of women came into the loos including Anna's best friend Jane. Josie hadn't realised that Jane was at the dinner and avoided the red head's eyes in the mirror. As she made to leave, Jane approached her and said, "Hi Josie, can I have a word?"

"Sure," she replied dreading what Jane had to say.

"Out here," the red head indicated, as if they were about to share a big secret.

The girls moved toward the corridor between the ladies and the main dining room. "Tell me to mind my own business, but what was all that about with Max and Lorenza earlier? I missed the episode but everyone is talking about it. I'm Anna's friend and she is really upset by this whole Max thing. I keep telling her what a shit he is but she still cares deeply for him. God knows why after the way he's treated her."

Josie didn't know what to say. She could easily lie to Jane but she didn't want to. She liked this woman who had a certain honesty and forthrightness about her that Josie admired. She didn't want Jane to think badly of her but if telling her meant more nails in the coffin for Max then so be it. Josie told her the whole story, starting with Longchamps and up to her plan for revenge this evening. She omitted the complication of Paul from the story, as that was unfair to him.

"Look Jane, I'm not proud of what I did and I really didn't want to hurt Anna but you know how Max is? He just bowled me over. I genuinely didn't know on that first evening that he even had a girlfriend and by the time I found out it was too late, I was hooked. I'm really sorry but I think Anna is far better off without him. Max is just one of these guys who thinks he can have his cake and eat it. He is a serial adulterer with no idea about loyalty or commitment. I can't ever see him changing. Max will always be chasing the next conquest.

"I know," replied Jane, "and I do understand Josie. Max tried it on with me once. He tried every trick in the book to get my panties off. Max was very persistent but I told him I'd tell Anna if he didn't back off. Our relationship was never the same after that. It was around the time we were planning Anna's surprise party, it was so difficult. I wasn't shocked to find out he'd been playing away, I just didn't realise quite how much."

Josie squirmed, she felt awful if not a bit relieved at telling Jane about Max. She asked her if she was planning on telling Anna. "I'm not sure, yet. If I do it could be difficult for you and Paul at other events here in the future. But I really want her to know what a bastard Max really is and not just to her. I think it's important to know that the affaire with Lorenza wasn't a one-off. Hopefully that will stop her pining over him."

Josie decided not to put Jane straight about her and Paul, it was just too complicated. Instead she said, "I don't mind if you tell Anna, Jane. In fact, I'd be happy to tell her myself. It's the least I can do after what I've done."

"We'll see. I'll play it by ear. Can I have your mobile number though? I'll give you call if Anna wants to see you, OK?"

"OK," replied Josie, hoping that Jane wouldn't call. "I'm glad I've told you Jane. I hope you can make Anna realise what sort of guy Max really is. I'm sure she will be much happier without him."

The girls entered the dining room together and Paul immediately rushed over. "Honestly Josie, I thought you'd done a runner on me. You've been gone ages."

Josie apologised and explained that she had been talking to Jane. She told Paul that she'd confessed to the whole sordid affair and that Jane might tell Anna.

"That was brave of you," he said, obviously surprised.

"Look Paul, I'm not proud of what happened and I have to live with that. Max is an out and out shit and the more people who know that the better. I do hope Jane tells Anna the whole story and I've even agreed to tell her myself if Jane thinks it's a good idea. I just want to draw a line under the whole sorry business and get on with my life."

Paul nodded but the sadness from earlier remained in his eyes. He knew she also meant to get on with her life without him.

The couple left shortly after the speeches and before the dancing began, Josie just wasn't in the mood. Paul dropped Josie off and she didn't invite him in. She watched the headlights of his car driving off down the street and felt a mix of relief and sadness. She knew they probably couldn't just be friends, but she could now move on. She had a good life, great friends and a new job to look forward to and for Josie that was enough for the moment.

Ellis Rose

ELLIS ROSE
ANOTHER NIGHT IN PARIS

With wicked Max well and truly out of the picture or so Josie hopes, after taking revenge in front of his new Spanish girlfriend. Josie's future is looking bright, with a new job and a new man in her life, Christian Lecourt. But things are never quite that simple.

Josie's new job at Renseignements, a glitzy boutique PR consultancy is put in jeopardy by a jealous colleague. Sally Marsden-Lloyd, a spoilt little rich girl who causes no end of conflict at work and has set her sights on taking Josie down. Both women desperately want to work on the prestigious Four Season's account, a major hotel group. When Helene Du Tilly, wife of the Managing Director and notorious for having numerous affairs with both men and women, favours Josie the scene is set for a Bataille Royale.

Chrissie's love life isn't going smoothly either. The reappearance of Claude's psycho ex-girlfriend Dominique throws a spanner in the works. When Claude and Christian are involved in a tragic car accident both young women find themselves having to deal with situations more complicated than they ever imagined.

For readers who love Jackie Collins, Jilly Cooper and enjoyed 50 Shades, you won't be disappointed by the latest bonkbuster from the author, Ellis Rose, Another Night in Paris. As the title suggests, the novel picks up from where One Night in Paris left off. Sexy English girl Josie James, the luscious centrefold, with little girl charm, a big girl body, and an appetite for all that Paris has to offer continues her raunchy, riotous exploits. This second novel in the trilogy offers a 'no holds barred' exploration of Josie and her friends tangled and graphic love lives.

ELLIS ROSE
LAST NIGHT IN PARIS

With Christian's slow recovery from a coma after the serious car accident, Josie finds herself torn between caring for her man and her career. The prestigious Four Seasons Pan-European launch is delicately poised and Josie is in the firing line if it all fails.

The pressures of juggling Christian with punishing hours and stress at work result in a major bust-up at Renseignements with Sally Marsden-Lloyd. This time Josie is not in a forgiving mood and the spoilt little rich girl may have bitten off more than she can swallow. The situation becomes impossible when a vile anonymous letter is circulated that accuses her of a sordid affair with her dishy boss Thomas, a serial womanizer. Valérie, his long suffering wife naturally goes ballistic and the agencies senior partner, Jacques Fredet is called upon to investigate the allegations.

Josie's wayward younger sister, Ella James proves an unwelcome distraction when she visits. Ella takes up with the intriguing but dangerous Luc de la Fontaine and goes missing on her final night in Paris. The glitzy Four Seasons event in Switzerland finally brings everything to a head and changes the path of Josie's life forever.

"A 'no holds barred' exploration of tangled and graphic love lives, perhaps no one plays with the heart – and other body parts – as successfully as the scandalous Ellis Rose."

WHAT THEY SAY ABOUT ELLIS ROSE

"A sexy, funny, riotous bonkbuster…Switch off your phone, grab a glass of bubbly and escape into an outrageous world of sex, thrills, glamour and passion. You'll be addicted…" AMAZON

"Packed full of sauciness, sex and intrigue, this lively romp takes you on a colourful journey through the sparkling world of Paris, from the ultra-highs to the face-planting lows. If you're looking for a sexy, racy, riotous read, this is the perfect choice…" AMAZON

"The sex scenes will make even the most frigid and puritanical of us aware that we are alive, and I suggest that if you have a partner, make sure they are available…you will want to do IT while reading. It is a sexy, thrilling, glitzy bonkbuster and is the most fun you can have between two covers…" AMAZON

"Fast, shameless and mesmeric fiction…offers an intoxicating blend of swooning romance, raunchy sex and agonising love stories…" GOODREADS

"A 'no holds barred' exploration of tangled and graphic love lives, perhaps no one plays with the heart – and other body parts – as successfully as the scandalous Ellis Rose." AMAZON

"Another Night… adult contemporary romance that contains strong sexual content and sultry raunchy thrills…inject some heat into your reading…" AMAZON

THE FINDING
ALAN M KEEF

Jennifer Suffram is the daughter of an old established but slightly down at heel Cotswold farming family. She feels stifled by her fiancé, the patronising Richard, the hum drum plod of her life and decides on a once in lifetime trip to East Africa in an effort to 'find herself'. Rather than finding herself she finds David, a handsome young man with a mysterious past.

But finding him upon her return to England is another matter entirely, with no contact details she turns sleuth and the couple are reunited. Despite their brief acquaintance, when he suffers a serious injury he calls for her help and in a matter of days she finds herself acting not only as his chauffeur and personal assistant but almost as his wife. And before she can stop herself, she's swept up in an affair so sensual she ignores all the warnings…

To her surprise she finds she likes the atmosphere and the people engaged in the family engineering business in Carlisle with the exception of David's PA, Muriel, with whom she is instantly at loggerheads. Jennifer's confrontations with Muriel unearth dark undercurrents of deception, menace and sex that cast light on some shocking skeletons buried in David's past. Can their fledgling romance withstand the revelations…?

"Wonderful dialogue, colourful characters, breathtaking twists and a plot that allows no pause for breath…all is perfectly weaved together to create an irresistible story in which absolutely nothing is as it seems" AMAZON

"An addictive novel to be devoured in one sitting…the plot rattles along with gusto…a real page-turner" AMAZON

PROPHECY OF RAVENS
KEN BLAKEMORE

KILLER BUG ESCAPES LAB

Authorities in the US have confirmed that the deadly virus now sweeping through California escaped from a laboratory.

LOCKED IN WITH THE PLAGUE

Five brave doctors, sixteen courageous nurses, ten plucky health workers are sacrificing their lives at the Princess Diana Hospital, Leeds, for us. By the time you read this, they may already have been taken by the Superflu plague sweeping through our country.

TWO MILLENNIA – AND NOW IT'S THE END

We knew it would happen. Great Britain's population has dwindled to a few million, as has almost every other country's. We knew there was no health service there and that all telecommunications, food supplies, the currency and the transport system had broken down. But we clung to hopes – hopes that one day the Old Country would rise again. That prospect now looks very remote indeed.

This is Britain sixty years from now – a land slowly recovering, like the rest of the world, from three devastating epidemics. It's an island of only a few million people. It faces the prospect of a slide back into a new medieval age: a land of dense forests, superstition and darkness – a land of ravens.

Lara Johnson is the youngest-ever high court judge to be appointed in the city of New Warwick. In the company of a young woman reporter, Star Edkin, Lara decides to set off on a final quest to find her missing husband. They travel through a country on the brink of rebellion and fraught with the dangers of a nuclear disaster.

"A genuinely unsettling dystopian novel…prescient to the degree that today's newspaper headlines accurately mirror the plot…an ambitious and addictive novel" SUE SAVITT, Faber & Faber

Ellis Rose